MW00914539

| | DATE DUE | | |
|---|---|---|---|
| MAY 2 6 2010 | | | |
| | | | |
| | | | |
| | | | |
| | | | 603 |
| | | | |
| | | | |
| | | | |
| | | | |
| | | | |
| | | | |

**Boswell Public Library**
580-566-2866

To

Jane Austen, thank you for creating these wonderful characters

**Enid Wilson** loves sexy romance. Her writing career began with a daily newspaper, writing educational advice for students. She then branches out into writing marketing materials and advertising copies. Enid's first paranormal novel *In Quest of Theta Magic*, received several top reviews. Enid can be contacted at enid.wilson28@yahoo.com.au or www.steamydarcy.com

Illustration by Z. Diaz

Cover design by Cloud Cat Graphics, www.cloudcat.com

First published 2009

BARGAIN WITH THE DEVIL © 2009 by Enid Wilson

# CHAPTER ONE

Elizabeth Bennet strolled slowly past a line of elegant townhouses in a fashionable area in London for the second day in a row, a maid following a few steps behind her. She knew that, unlike her normal joyful countenance, her face must look pale and agitated. Then, suddenly, her spirits brightened. Increasing her pace, she walked almost directly into the path of a tall gentleman.

"Mr. Darcy!"

"Miss Bennet!"

"Pray forgive me! I was not looking where I was heading. It was a lovely day and I was hoping to shop at Bond Street but I could not resist taking a walk to admire the lovely townhouses in the area."

"How long have you been in London, Miss Bennet?"

"But two days, sir."

"Where are you staying?"

"At my aunt and uncle's."

"But of course. I...am walking to my club. Is your family in good health?"

Elizabeth walked closer to him and lowered her voice. "I fear we are very ill indeed, Mr. Darcy. May I interrupt your day and request a more private meeting with you, in the park around the corner?"

She saw his eyes widened. He nodded his head and said, for the benefit of the footman and maid who looked on, "Miss Bennet, it was a pleasure to meet you in London again. May I escort you to Bond Street through the park?" He then offered her his arm.

"My pleasure," she replied and gave him a small smile. When she put her hand on his arm, she could feel the strength and the warmth of his arm, even through the thick coat. She shivered.

"Are you cold, Miss Bennet?"

"No," she declared stubbornly, "I am well."

Mr. Fitzwilliam Darcy cast her a look. They walked on silently while her maid followed.

"Should we take a rest over there?" He asked at last.

His deep voice startled Elizabeth from her dark thoughts. With a sigh, she took a seat at a bench under a large Chestnut tree. He sat down, as well, at the far end of the bench, while her maid wandered farther.

The park was small, and there were few people present, due no doubt to the early morning hour.

Elizabeth gathered her thoughts. "Mr. Darcy, pray excuse my impertinence for requesting this private meeting with you."

He did not reply but turned slightly to glance at her.

Bracing herself, Elizabeth began. "I would like to apologise for abusing you so abominably to your face in Hunsford, all the more so because my behaviour was based on untrue facts. I am truly ashamed of myself. My actions were blind, partial, prejudiced and absurd."

"Miss Bennet…"

"Pray allow me to continue, Mr. Darcy. Vanity has been my folly. From the very outset of our acquaintance, I was pleased with the preference of Mr. Wickham, and offended by your seeming neglect. I have courted prepossession and ignorance, driving reason away where either of you were concerned. Till the moment I read your letter, I never knew myself."

"Pray do not..."

"And now, the most dreadful circumstance has overtaken our family." Tears sprang to her eyes despite her determined efforts to compose herself. "My younger sister, Lydia, has left all her friends, and has eloped, throwing herself into the power of…of Mr. Wickham."

For a terrible instant, Darcy appeared fixed in astonishment. Then he stood up and paced before her. "How did it happen?" he prompted tersely.

Elizabeth drew a steadying breath, determined to respond in as controlled a manner as possible. "The militia left Meryton about the same time as I left for Hunsford. My sister Lydia was invited by Colonel Forster's wife to stay with her for a few weeks. Lydia left Brighton together with Mr. Wickham on Sunday night, and they were traced almost to London, but not beyond."

"What has been done? What has been attempted, to recover her?"

"My father is here in London. He has been trying to find her for the past three days, with my uncle's assistance. He sent for me from Kent at the same time. That was the reason I requested this meeting. You have known Mr. Wickham since your youth. I beg for intelligence to help us in our search."

Mr. Darcy made no answer. He continued to pace for a while, then stopped and looked sharply at her.

Elizabeth returned his gaze through teary eyes.

"And what would be my reward for helping you?" He asked at last.

It was Elizabeth's turn to widen her eyes. "Reward? I am appealing to your gentleman's nature to help a family in distress."

He laughed coolly. "As I recall, you stated yourself that I had a selfish disdain for the feelings of others, and that I was no gentleman. Why would such a man help a family in distress without some reward in view?"

"But you are a man of fortune. What more...?" Elizabeth's trembling voice faded. Standing abruptly, she said to him coldly, "It was a mistake for me to beg you for intelligence. Mr. Darcy, pray forgive me for interrupting your day."

She began to walk away, but he grabbed her arm and prevented her retreat. "Sit down, Miss Bennet. You can ill afford to be missish when I can help you recover Miss Lydia and force Wickham to marry her."

She stared at him in disbelief. "You cannot seriously suggest that I would trade my virtue for it. How can you believe that I would corrupt the reputation of our family just to save it from another form of ruination?"

"You are so certain that I demand you to sell your soul?"

Elizabeth faltered. "But…if you are not asking me to be your…your mistress, pray tell what other reward were you hoping for?"

Maddeningly, he spread his hands. "In truth, I did not have a specific goal in mind when I asked. I was simply inquiring. But since you are already thinking in that direction…"

"Mr. Darcy! Pray do not toy with me," she protested, her throat aching with distress. "My family is in ruin. I have no heart for playing such games with you."

"So, you admit that you were always playing games with me, in the past? Was that why you thought that the pain of your rejection would be of only short duration? You thought I was devoid of true feelings in the matter?"

"I have apologised for hurting you…"

"No, you have only apologised for abusing me to my face. You did not take my feelings seriously when you refused my offer, nor have you indicated that you do so even now, with your apology."

"Sir, if you want me to apologise for hurting your feelings…"

"There is no point in an apology if the need for issuing one did not even occur to you before I mentioned it."

"What do you want then? I cannot conceive that you would want me as your wife now, even if you should offer your support to us, for you must realise that I would be a sister to Mr. Wickham. Moreover, you have just stated that you do not want me as your mistress – not that I would agree to such a situation in any event. So tell me, please, what kind of reward you could possibly have in mind, considering that you know my family not to be in any way capable of offering financial recompense to you."

His shoulders lifted fractionally and fell. "I do not know yet. Can we not simply agree that you will owe me some reward if I succeed in finding your sister? I can promise that I shall not offer you the arrangement of a mistress. Other than that, I would consider myself at liberty to ask you to do whatever I wish, as reward."

"But that is the vaguest term of agreement! What if you should request that I do something immoral?"

His face was stern with offended pride. "Is your opinion of me so low that you believe me capable of asking you to do something immoral? If so, I am grieved indeed."

Cheeks aflame, she protested, "No, sir, I am not saying that I believe you would. But surely we should not enter a bargain without the clearest terms in mind."

"You are a worthy opponent in negotiation. How, then, does this suit you? I shall bring my sister to walk in the park tomorrow, at the same hour as today. At that time, I shall introduce her to you so that I may contact you through her, thereafter, without raising undue suspicion." He raised a single brow. "And I shall wait to name my reward until after I have succeeded in arranging for Wickham to marry your sister."

"What, then, if I refuse to grant your reward?"

His expression hardened. "Then I will simply undo the arrangements."

Elizabeth gasped. "But that is no negotiation at all, if I do not have the right to refuse!"

"You cannot refuse. You can, however, negotiate." Darcy's dark gaze challenged her. "So then, do we have an agreement?"

Returning his glare, she nodded reluctantly.

*** 

The following day, true to his agreement, Mr. Darcy and his sister encountered Elizabeth. "Miss Bennet, what a coincidence! Are you walking to Bond Street again?"

"Why, Mr. Darcy, you have caught me once again. Some ladies just cannot stay away from the shops."

"May I introduce my sister?"

"My pleasure."

"Miss Bennet, this is my sister, Georgiana, and her companion, Mrs. Annesley. Georgiana, this is Miss Bennet from Hertfordshire. I made her acquaintance when I last stayed with Bingley at Netherfield."

"Miss Darcy and Mrs. Annesley, it is a pleasure to meet you. Miss Darcy, I have heard that you sing and play the pianoforte very well."

Elizabeth conversed with Miss Darcy for some moments before her brother invited his sister to take a rest with Mrs. Annesley on the bench under the Chestnut tree while he strolled on with Elizabeth.

"I have intelligence on where they are," he said without prologue, as soon as they were relatively alone.

"So soon?" Her pulse quickened. "Can we arrange for my father or uncle to be with you when you confront them?"

"It is not advisable. I do not want your family to call Wickham out. They may be hurt."

"But surely they can help in some way."

"Once I reach the couple and have negotiated with Wickham, I will talk to your uncle and ask him to take the credit for their discovery, so long as he does not raise the matter with your father."

"But why? Why must there be secrecy with my father?"

Mr. Darcy gave her a long-suffering look. "Would you be eager to explain to your father how you begged for my assistance? Or how you settled upon some future reward with me? If so, I am certain that he will be calling *me* out, instead."

"Then how do you propose to explain all of this to my uncle?"

"You will have to trust me, and arrange a time for me to call upon your uncle at his warehouse. From there, I will do my part."

"How did you know that my uncle has a warehouse?"

"I make it my business to know about those with whom I am dealing, especially when it comes to any kind of business venture."

\*\*\*

A few days later, Mr. Bennet said to his brother, "Edward, you must tell me how much you have laid down to bring this about. I have to work out a plan to repay you."

"No, Thomas, do not distress yourself. I had a very fine year with my investments. I would not do it if I could not afford it." Mr. Gardiner replied.

"Wickham is a fool if he takes Lydia for a farthing less than ten thousand pounds."

Elizabeth exclaimed, "Ten thousand pounds? Heaven forbid! How is half such a sum to be repaid?"

Her father ignored her outburst. "Edward, Lydia is my daughter. I am utterly ashamed of myself for not thinking ahead sufficiently to save up enough money to bribe some worthless young men into marrying my silly daughters. Now I am depleting your children's inheritance for my own stupidity."

"Thomas, do not speak of it any more. Lydia is my relation, too. We cannot see her ruined. Besides, we are all family and I fear it would darken the reputation of my children, as well."

The two gentlemen clasped hands. "Edward, you are a good man. I shall think up some way to repay you, though it may be slowly done."

Touched, Elizabeth smiled upon them both. "Papa, you look exhausted. I'm certain that Uncle Edward will understand if you retire now."

Wearily, Mr. Bennet agreed.

As he left the room, Elizabeth said quietly, "Uncle, might I take up just a bit more of your time, to discuss the wedding arrangements for Lydia and Mr. Wickham?"

He acquiesced, and they resumed their seats by the fire.

Elizabeth addressed him, filled with dread, "Uncle Edward, can it possibly be true that Mr. Darcy has laid down over ten thousand pounds over this matter?"

Her uncle sighed. "No, not as much as all that, although it is quite bad enough. It is my understanding that he has put forth roughly five thousand pounds."

"Five thousands pounds," Elizabeth echoed despondently "Mr. Darcy did not agree for us to settle it?"

"He argued that this lamentable situation arose because of his reserve and his want of proper consideration. It allowed

Wickham's character to be so badly misunderstood, causing the blackguard to be received and noticed as he was."

"How could Mr. Darcy blame himself for such a rake's misdeeds?"

Her uncle shook his head. "Perhaps there was some small measure of truth in it. But in spite of all this fine talking, my dear Lizzy, I would never have yielded if I had not thought he had another interest in the affair. I do not speak it to be grateful, for I would most readily have settled the entire amount myself."

"What can you possibly mean, Uncle, by 'another interest in the affair'?"

"Well, Mr. Darcy was perfectly well-behaved, polite and unassuming during our meeting. I actually thought him rather sly. He hardly ever mentioned your name. But every time he did, I could see that he had your best interests at heart. Indeed, he has invited us to stay at his estate of Pemberley when we tour the North, come this summer."

"I thought we were going to the Lakes." Elizabeth blushed at the thought of staying at Pemberley. Was that the reward that Mr. Darcy had settled upon?

"I was convinced to make the detour by Mr. Darcy, and of course your aunt agreed, as she would enjoy visiting Lambton, the town where she grew up. It is just five miles from Pemberley. We will stay there for some three weeks."

*Three weeks in Mr. Darcy's house! What does he want with me?* Elizabeth thought, and felt a ribbon of heat rise through her.

\*\*\*

The next day, Mr. Darcy came to discuss his reward.

He did indeed make it his business to know those with whom he was dealing. He came to call upon Elizabeth when her father and uncle were away, consulting with their lawyers.

Lydia was still upstairs in her bedroom, but Elizabeth and her aunt received Mr. Darcy, his sister and her companion. After a few pleasantries, he managed to draw her to sit aside from the others. In a low voice, he confided, "I have come to discuss my reward."

Elizabeth looked at her hands, folded neatly in her lap. "Well?"

"I want…to spend some time with you."

"Spend some time?" she repeated softly. "What do you mean?"

"I shall explain to Bingley that I was wrong about Miss Bennet when he returns to London, next week. With luck, he will not be too angry with me, and will invite my sister and I to journey to Hertfordshire for a few weeks. I plan to do so, after Wickham and his wife leave the vicinity."

"You would do that? Speak to Mr. Bingley about Jane?"

"I always try to correct what I have made wrong. And I imagine, by now, that you have heard from your uncle about my invitation to them – and to you – to pass time at Pemberley in the summer?"

"Yes, for three weeks."

"After your visit to Pemberley, you could return the favour and invite my sister and I to Longbourn for Christmas."

"You want to stay with my family during Christmas?"

"Well, perhaps a happy event will have happened before then and I can stay in Netherfield. If not, I will be happy to stay in Longbourn."

"What...what exactly will we do when we...spend some time together?"

"I intend to make my ardent admiration more thoroughly known to you," Mr. Darcy leaned forward and murmured, and Elizabeth could feel his breath hot against the bare skin of her neck.

"Nothing immoral, remember," Elizabeth cautioned breathlessly.

"Everything will be designed for your pleasure."

Elizabeth's eyes widened, and a retort rose to her lips. She saw Mr. Darcy turn his head and dart a glance at those on the opposite side of the room. Assured that no one was watching them, he took her hand, raised it to his lips, kissed the inside of her wrist, then allowed the tip of his tongue to caress the soft flesh there before biting it lightly.

For Elizabeth, it felt as if a thunderbolt had coursed through her body. Her intended retort was lost as she held her breath, determined not to make a sound that might alert the others in the room to the liberty he took.

Mr. Darcy gave her a devilish smile, straightened, and signaled for his sister and her companion to prepare to take their leave, Thereby neatly avoiding any response that Elizabeth might have been tempted to express.

*Oh my Lord!* Elizabeth thought wildly as she watched him take his leave, *what have I just agreed to reward him with?*

# CHAPTER TWO

"Father! Father! It's Lydia!" Elizabeth cried out as she rushed down to the morning room.

"My dear, whatever is the matter?" Mr. Bennet replied. He had awakened early and was breaking his fast alone at the Gardiner's townhouse. The Gardiners themselves had gone out. Lydia's wedding was scheduled for two days hence. Mr. Bennet longed to finish the whole sorry business and return to his beloved library at Longbourn as soon as humanly possible.

"Father, Lydia has run away with Mr. Wickham again."

"Again? Whatever do you mean by that?"

"She left a letter. She states that Mr. Wickham does not like the commission in the North that Uncle Gardiner purchased for him. She says that they will marry and move to Bath instead; and that she will be in contact with us after she settled down."

"The worthless young man! He is after more money, I am certain. I shall..." Mr. Bennet rose from his seat, appearing ready to breathe fire at Wickham, if necessary. A moment later, however, he clutched his chest, and collapsed onto the chair again.

"Father!" Elizabeth cried out.

***

Mr. Darcy received news of Wickham's disappearance early in the morning, and came to the Gardiner's townhouse with the hope of gaining a private meeting with its owner. Instead, he found Mr. Bennet collapsed in the morning room. The distressing news of his youngest daughter disappearing again had put such a strain on Mr. Bennet's heart that, although he was still breathing, he was unconscious.

Mr. Darcy assessed the situation and immediately took charge. He picked up the sick man and called out to a servant to direct him to Mr. Bennet's bedroom. He further instructed the servant to fetch his own private doctor.

Throughout the entire incident, Elizabeth could only stand by, watching Darcy's solicitous actions through tear-blurred eyes. He was gentle and decisive with her father, and polite to every one, even the servants. *Surely he would treat me with honour and decency. Oh, how now are we to find Lydia?*

Mr. Gardiner returned to a house of unhappy chaos. Mr. Darcy gained his immediate attention for a private meeting and they shut themselves up in the study for the better part of half an hour. Before the gentleman left, however, Elizabeth was able to corner Mr. Darcy in private at the hallway landing.

"Sir, I must thank you for your quick action in sending for the doctor. You may have saved my father's life."

He did not say anything but nodded his head, looking grave.

"What are we to do now?"

"Wickham left me a note. I shall take care of the matter."

"What does he want now?"

"I shall take care of it. You are not to worry."

"I insist! This concerns my family."

With a sigh, Mr. Darcy yielded. "He has demanded a further five thousand pounds and a townhouse in Stoke Newington. He says he will contact me once I settle the terms with his lawyer. He has given me five days to arrange it."

"Another five thousand pounds? Dear Heaven, what greed! How could Lydia be so stupid! What does he threaten to do if we cannot comply?"

"I shall speak to my steward. You must not distress yourself."

"But you cannot provide for him endlessly. The scoundrel! We must find them, and force him to marry Lydia. If we sent them off to one of the colonies, perhaps that would help us to forget all about them, so that Mr. Wickham could never trouble us again." Anger grew in Elizabeth's chest.

"The innkeeper where Wickham stayed overheard him stating that he did not intend to leave for Bath."

"But where, then, would they go?"

"I know Mrs. Younge has a sister in a fishing village not far from Dover and Wickham had been there before. I shall investigate that area."

"Might Uncle Edward go with you?"

"I believe your uncle has other more pressing obligations to fulfill, do you not agree? He must inform your mother about your father's condition, and speak with his steward in your father's absence."

"Then…may I go with you?"

"Absolutely not. It is not an area fit for a gentlewoman."

"But…"

"Elizabeth, you must keep your end of our bargain, and I shall keep mine! Now go back to your father. I will send news as soon as there is any to tell."

Mr. Darcy moved towards the door but Elizabeth blocked his way, insinuating her small body in front of his tall one. "I must help in the search. I am determined!" she said, her eyes ablaze as she challenged him.

But a matching determination had arisen in Darcy. He already blamed himself for not keeping a closer eye on Wickham, nor was he prepared to deal with a hot-headed woman breathing annoyance down his neck. "And how, pray tell, do you intend to handle a lowly man from a disreputable area?" He proceeded to demonstrate his meaning by wrapping his left arm around her waist and pulling her body hard against his. He looked straight down into her fiery gaze, warning her silently to back away.

She was standing on tiptoe, her body pressed against the length of his. She felt flustered and she sensed a hot flush rising onto her face. The bite he had given her on the wrist had only disappeared the night before, and now he was imprinting his shape on hers. Her breath grew quick and shallow, but she would not back away. "My courage rises with each new attempt to intimidate me."

Further incensed by her attitude, Mr. Darcy lowered his head and whispered into her ear, "Such a man would not be content with intimidation. He would do what I have wanted to do with you every time I have been in your presence, these past months." He positioned his right hand over her bosom, then squeezed it hard. Anticipating her scream, he was able to muffle it with a kiss, his tongue thrusting between her parted lips.

Elizabeth could not believe that two people could be this close. She felt she could not breathe, with his tongue playing havoc inside her mouth. Passion exploded in her chest as he fondled her roughly. Blood drained from her head down into her body, and she nearly swooned.

Abruptly, he released her and backed away, saying coarsely, "Learn from this lesson! Do not attempt anything hasty. I will send word once I know anything of importance." He whirled away and departed from the townhouse, leaving a weakened Elizabeth still plastered against the wall in a heated daze.

*** 

An hour later, however, Elizabeth felt ready to *brave the lion* again. Her uncle had left for Longbourn earlier, promising to inform Mrs. Bennet of the bad turn in her husband's health and to arrange business matters with her husband's steward. Elizabeth informed her aunt that Mr. Darcy would be going off to search for Lydia and Wickham, and then added that he had requested that Elizabeth stay with his sister while he was away, since Miss Darcy's companion had been called away suddenly.

Departing the house, Elizabeth trusted that her aunt would continue to believe her tale and would not question the matter further.

Arriving at Darcy's townhouse, she requested a private meeting with Miss Darcy, where she stated boldly that she and Mr. Darcy had been secretly engaged since their Easter meeting at Rosings. Since Darcy had already shared some of the particulars about Lydia and Wickham's situation, Elizabeth was able to persuade Georgiana to agree that she must accompany Mr. Darcy in his search for the wayward pair.

At first, Miss Darcy did not feel right about helping her secretly, but Elizabeth convinced the girl that she feared that Mr. Darcy might challenge Mr. Wickham to a duel, and that she believed that only her presence would prevent it. She also called upon Georgiana to agree, at need, to corroborate the story she had told to Mrs. Gardiner.

In turn, the young lady suggested sending a maid to Gracechurch Street to help care for Mr. Bennet in the meantime, and made enquiries with the footman about her brother's plan. They learned that he had ordered two hire coaches and had several servants ready for the journey. They would stay in Whitstable, a small coast town near Dover. He would then change into labourer's clothes and walk to the nearby fishing village from there on a 'private matter.'

"Why does my brother wish to go to the village himself, instead of sending the servants?" Miss Darcy asked.

"I believe he is determined to confront Mr. Wickham himself. That is why I fear that a duel may be imminent. I do not want him hurt. You must help me, Georgiana. You must!"

This last argument persuaded Georgiana to help her. So determined, the two women then dressed Elizabeth as one of Darcy's footman and slipped her in the front of one of the carriages after Darcy was onboard.

*** 

By the time the coaches arrived in Whitstable, the sun had set.

Mr. Darcy bid his men goodbye. The first village was about two miles away, on an isolated part of the shore. If the enquiry was not long, he hoped to be back to Whitstable before the night was out.

A few metres behind, Elizabeth followed him quietly, able to trail him on level ground. When he took the downward track by the river towards the sea, however, she had more difficulty keeping up with his pace. The growing darkness hindered her progress, as well. A few moments into her downward descent, she encountered a  slither of loose rock underfoot, and yelped aloud as it tumbled her down the bank to sprawl in the shallows of the slow-moving river.

Mr. Darcy heard a cry and turned back to find what looked like a slim lad sat in the shallow water. The boy had a smear of dirt on his face, and was staring at him with very bright eyes. In fact, those eyes looked very like…

"Elizabeth!"

"Mr. Darcy," Elizabeth acknowledged weakly. She had hurt her ankle, and her clothes were soaked. When she tried to stand, the injured leg gave way and she slipped again.

Mr. Darcy moved quickly toward her. Before he could grab her, she slipped back into the water and splashed more of it on both of them.

"I told you that this was no place for a gentlewoman! Why did you not listen to reason?" Darcy hissed.

"I do not want you to call Mr. Wickham out. And I desperately want to help you with Lydia. I know my sister, and you will need me to reckon with her. Besides, I am no gentlewoman now," she said, gesturing down at her boy's clothing.

"But you have injured your foot. Now I shall have to carry you the two miles back to Whitstable. Stubborn woman! You are hindering the search, rather than helping it."

Before they could argue further, they heard the approaching sound of men singing. Quickly, Darcy motioned for her to climb up and ride upon his back, with her arms wrapped around his neck, and her legs around his waist. At her scandalised look, he explained curtly that it was how a big brother would aid an injured younger brother.

"Wat yer doin' 'ere, mate?"

"My cousin and I were heading to Whitstable, but he fell and hurt his foot in the river just now." Mr. Darcy said.

"Whitstable be two miles on. Storm's a comin'. Ye'd best stay till mornin'. My brother, John, has a hut at Herne Bay that'd be closer. Stay there, if y'like."

Darcy looked up to the sky and agreed. He nodded and followed the men along the river to the sea, where they were taken to the hut of one of the fishermen. His family shared the hut with his brother and his wife. Darcy and Elizabeth were given the brother's room. The bed filled up most of the space in the room, without even a chair to sit on.

John's wife, Margaret, asked to have their wet clothes laid out for drying, and gave them trousers to wear for the time being. Inside the room, Elizabeth's face turned bright red. She could not wear nothing but trousers, and yet she could not refuse to give Margaret her clothes. It would look too suspicious. Mortified, she looked at the bed and whispered to Mr. Darcy, "Pray, turn your back. I will remove my clothing and stay in the bed. You shall give the clothes to Margaret for drying. You must plead a headache for me, as I have no clothes that will permit me to go outside."

Mr. Darcy turned his back and listened to the slithering noises behind him until Elizabeth said he could turn around. The wet clothes she had worn were now draped on the edge of the bed, and she had lain out another long piece of cloth near the window. She was lying under the bed sheet, and had pulled it up all the way to her neck.

Mr. Darcy said, "Should I not take that piece of cloth by the window out to Margaret as well?"

"No, she would find it strange that I possess such a piece of clothing."

"Why?"

"I used it to…"

"To what?"

"To bind my bosom."

"Oh!" Darcy exclaimed, flustered by the thought of her binding up her beautiful breasts. He said quickly, "It is you who must close your eyes now. I need to change."

Elizabeth closed her eyes, silently listening as he removed his wet clothes and donned the dry ones. "I am finished." He said.

When she opened her eyes, she wished she had not. Although she was a country girl, and had seen many farmers without their shirts working in the hot sun, she was not prepared for the sight of a shirtless Mr. Darcy. His body was nothing like that of most farmers. His chest looked smooth and muscular. He was about to collect all of the clothes to leave the room when Elizabeth called out to him in a low voice.

"Mr. Darcy, you will not do."

Darcy turned to look at her.

"You do not look like a labourer," she confided.

He looked at his trousers and said, "These are a fisherman's trousers, though too short for me." He must be five inches taller than the owner of the clothes. Elizabeth could see that much of his calf exposed by each pant leg.

Colouring, she tried again. "I mean…your chest. You look… too clean and tidy."

"Oh!" He looked around the room and spotted a broken bucket of herbs on the window sill. Scooping up a handful of dirt, he smeared some of it judiciously on his face, chest and exposed legs.

Elizabeth was mesmerised by his actions. She felt as if she were spying on him, as if he was taking a bath, a dirty bath.

"Will I do now?" he asked.

"Yes." She averted her gaze and whispered shyly.

Looking reassured, he nodded his thanks curtly and left her there.

\*\*\*

To Elizabeth's surprise, Mr. Darcy returned shortly with a small meal for her, and then left the room again, informing her calmly that John and the other fishermen had invited him to join them for a drink.

The sounds of a storm raged outside the hut. Elizabeth was exhausted after her traumatic day. She could hear the men's loud talking and singing outside her bedroom for endless hours. She reminded herself that she would need to collect the cloth by the window, as soon as it was less wet, so that she could bind herself again. She felt exposed lying on the bed, wearing only a pair of borrowed trousers, but she was too tired to move. Finally, she closed her eyes, intending to do so only for a moment...and was startled to awaken with a warm body by her side. Darcy was stretched beside her, his arm draped over her waist. His face was nestled close to hers. And he smelt of alcohol.

"Mr. Darcy! What are you doing in my bed?" Elizabeth whispered in agitation, trying to push him away.

Drowsily, Darcy replied, "Sleeping. The bed fills...the whole room. Where else can I sleep but here on the bed?"

"But you are most improperly attired!"

"As are you, since they gave us no shirts." Instead of releasing her, he brushed his splayed fingers over her breasts. "Your skin is so smooth, Elizabeth. I love your...bosom. I have wanted to touch and kiss your...breasts for so long, as earlier as when we were at...Netherfield." His hand rubbed around the creamy mound in a circular motion. "Firm and pert." His fingers plucked at her nipple. "Like a rock! How I long to...suckle it, as I have done in my dreams."

Elizabeth could scarcely believe that he had had such thoughts about her so early in their acquaintance. His hand and fingers were creating sensations in her body which she had never before experienced. She glowed with warmth and felt a tingling wetness gathering between her legs. However, her years of training in how to properly behave as a gently bred lady would not let her allow him to continue to take such liberties. She pushed his hand away and said breathlessly, "Mr. Darcy, you are drunk! Go to sleep."

A drunken Darcy seemed far more obedient than the sober counterpart with whom she was used to dealing. He stopped caressing her. But he seemed more inclined than usual to talk as well. He murmured, "Cheap alcohol would not make me drunk. I am simply feeling...happy. Did you know that Whitstable is famous for its...oysters? They tell me that oysters are good for the men. It makes them go…on and on. You know, on and on…with their women. Do you want to try?

"No? …Ah well, we could not…try it anyway. All of the oysters are for sale. The fishermen are not allowed to eat their catch. These particular fishermen are really surprisingly nice. We talked and sang. I did not know I had such a…baritone voice. Do you want to hear me sing? … No? …You know, John was telling me that I should teach you better manners."

"Manners…?! Whyever were you talking about me in such a regard?"

"They said you seemed like a…milksop, hiding your face against the back of…my neck while we were walking down to the sea, and claiming that a…headache prevented you from coming out to drink with us. I told them that my…cousin was young and innocent, and that I did not want them to…corrupt him, just yet." Mr. Darcy chuckled, seeming to like his own joke.

"You know perfectly well why I could not go out," Elizabeth hissed.

"Well yes, *you* know, and *I* know, but *they* do not know. They were really quite…amusing. They said I should…teach you how to scratch your bulge. Start young, scratch young, and the bulge will…grow larger." He laughed again.

"Mr. Darcy, you are drunk! This is not a discussion you should be conducting with a lady."

"Ah, but you said yourself that you were…not a lady now. And I told you already that I am not drunk. I can still teach you how to…scratch. I know how to do it, though I do not do it as…often as they do. And, of course, I only do it…in private. Still, I can instruct you."

"No!" Elizabeth protested, but she felt him take her hand and pull it down to the front of her trousers. She tried to struggle free but he was too strong.

"Now, scratch like this. All men must…do this, once in awhile, or else they do not look…manly." As Elizabeth's hand hung resolutely limp, he used his own fingertips to scratch lightly at the fabric between her legs. Elizabeth felt her blood draining from her head, rushing down to the area beneath his touch.

"Got that? Good. And when you…sit, you must sit with legs apart. The wider…you part your legs, the bigger…you imply your bulge to be. Then the others will see your manly assets."

"Mr. Darcy, indeed, you quite forget yourself!"

"Up!" Darcy sat up and pulled the bed sheet away, then tugged at Elizabeth to sit on the edge of the bed.

Shocked, she tried to cover her breasts.

"That is…no way for a man to sit," Darcy insisted, and parted her legs. "Yes, men sit like that, with legs apart."

Elizabeth struggled, trying to cross her legs, but he would not have it. He arranged her limbs once again, in the position he liked. "Now, that is it." He stopped and peered at her in the darkness. "But I fear you still look like…a milksop." He moved his hand, tracing his fingers over her naked chest. "You have a bosom! Definitely a milksop!" Abruptly, his hand dropped, and he pushed her down to lie back on the bed. Elizabeth was afraid of what he might do next, but she heard him murmur, "Now sleep." He pulled the bed sheet up to cover them both, then hugged her tight, his hands caressing her naked flesh while he whispered to her ear, "I do love you, Elizabeth." Then his breathing became deep and even as he finally fell soundly to sleep.

# CHAPTER THREE

Elizabeth could not fall asleep with Mr. Darcy hugging her so tightly. His hot breath blew near her earlobe; his manly, woody scent flooded her nostrils, sending shivers down her spine. From time to time, his hands would slide over her body, caressing her flesh, making her tremble with delightful yet disturbing new sensations. His legs were tangled with hers, transferring heat to her core.

She thought back over recent events: his surprise proposal in Hunsford; their angry exchange; his letter; the dreadful news about Lydia's elopement; her plea for his help; his devilish demand for a reward; the relief of finding her sister; the second disappearance of the greedy pair; her father's collapse; and, finally, her decision to follow him in his search.

*Did I act in a flirtatious manner at Netherfield or in Kent? Did I falsely lead him into falling in love with me? How could he love me without conversing much with me? How could I not have known of his intention? Was my reproof at his proposal too harsh? How could I not have been harsh? He was truly arrogant, conceited and insensitive to the feelings of all others in Meryton.*

*What about the astonishment, apprehension and even horror which oppressed me when I read his letter? How could I have been so mistaken about his character? And what of his compliment to me? He appeared to truly admire me. And his shocking claim for recompense! I shall never debase myself to become his mistress. And yet he shall not want to marry me now. What did he mean by wanting to make his ardent admiration more thoroughly known by me? Does he desire to make me love him and then suffer at his rejection?*

*Was I wrong to follow him? He will undoubtedly be furious when he finds out what I told Georgiana. Was I attempting to force his hand by telling his sister we were secretly engaged? What else could I have done? I felt certain he would call the scoundrel out. How could I allow him to be harmed? Am I really hindering the search?*

*There is also this situation here. We are spending a night together, in the same bed. He has seen and touched my body. I am truly compromised. Does he still desire to marry me?*

*And do I truly wish to marry him, if he still has the same feelings for me? I know now that it was he who was wronged by Mr. Wickham, not the other way around. He has promised to rectify the situation with Jane and Bingley. And he was not arrogant to Uncle's servants. What, if anything, do I still hold against him?*

*By following him today, I have taken the decision out of his hands. If he is honourable, he will have to ask for my hand again. Did I underestimate his love for me? Would it be of long duration? Was he just being honest when he told me he overcame tremendous objections to ask for my hand? And when he kissed and ... caressed me, my heart seemed to burst out and my blood felt inflamed within my body. Oh, his mouth, his tongue, his hands – they were like magic! But how can I think about these things when Lydia is still lost? Am I as wanton and undisciplined as my sister?*

*I had never supposed Mr. Darcy to have a humorous side, teaching me to scratch myself and part my legs. It was embarrassing...and yet, I must admit, quite hilarious. Indeed, I cannot help grinning now, thinking of the haughty Mr. Darcy scratching himself in private. He probably will not remember what happened when he wakes up tomorrow, or will not admit it, if he does. He is usually far too serious for his own good. It would be a pleasure to teach him to take life less seriously and to enjoy making gentle sport of both our neighbours and ourselves. Am I the right person to teach him?*

The hour was late indeed when, after exploring ever more pleasant thoughts about Mr. Darcy, Elizabeth finally fell asleep.

\*\*\*

When Darcy woke up to the light of the next day's dawn, he felt heavy headed. Slowly, he remembered the events the day before: finding the distasteful note from Wickham, Mr. Bennet's collapse, the private meeting with Mr. Gardiner, and the kiss at the Gardiner's townhouse.

*Yes, that hot, rough, punishing kiss I bestowed upon her. I can still feel the sensation of connecting to her mouth and pleasuring her body. The stubborn woman! She ignored my warning completely! Why has she followed me? Does she not have any respect for my word? Does she not trust my abilities at all?*

He remembered seeing her lying on the bed at the fishermen's hut, her body covered by the bed sheet. *My drinking and singing, did it happen? I was singing with the fishermen. And then...what followed next? I cannot remember clearly...*

A faint lavender smell tantalised his senses. He could feel his head on a soft, moving...was it really a moving pillow?

When he raised his body and looked down at the ... pillow, his eyes widened. It was Elizabeth's bosom! Her naked bosom had been his pillow for the night. He swallowed against the sudden tightness in his throat. Then, unable to help himself, he pulled the bed sheet lower, allowing the brightening sunlight to display her treasures.

The hat she had worn had become dislodged in the course of the night, and her hair escaped the bounds of its pins. With her dishevelled tresses framing her lovely face, she looked young and adorable.

And her breasts! Darcy swallowed again, totally mesmerised by the sight. Even though faint traces of dirt were smeared here and there over the porcelain smoothness of her skin, she could hardly have appeared more desirable to him. Her steady breathing thrust her bosom up and down, drawing his attention to her twin peaks.

He had long imagined devouring her body in his dreams. Now that he could do so freely, he could not seem to take the final step across the boundary. Taking a deep breath and calming himself, he held out his hand, wanting to caress her bosom. But before his fingertips could reach her enticing body, he withdrew his hand, folding it tightly into a fist at his side. Still, the temptation was very great indeed. He teased the bed sheet down further, gazing at her smooth, slender abdomen. When he drew the sheet a few inches lower, he encountered the sight of her trousers!

Remembering the other incidence, he raised his hands to cradle his muzzy head. *Dear Heaven, did I actually instruct her on how to scratch 'her' bulge, and teach her to sit with her legs apart? Oh, Lord, how can I ever remedy my shameful behaviour? Getting drunk and talking ridiculously is bound to have destroyed the last of her respect of me, if she ever truly had any for me at all.*

He lay back down on the bed, not daring to touch her. His mind was filled with embarrassment about the incidence and regret for drinking too much. He thought back with despair over recent events: the disastrous proposal in Hunsford; the letter; their meeting in the park; the search for Wickham; his audacious demand for reward.

*How could I get everything so wrong? I was so certain she was hoping for and expecting my address. But, in fact, she felt that I was the last man in the world whom she could ever be prevailed upon to marry! How could she not have noticed the attention and honour I bestowed upon her? I danced with no one but her at the Netherfield ball! I found every opportunity to meet up with her during her rambles at Rosings. How could she think that the pain of her rejection would be of only short duration for me? I shall never forget her words: "Had you behaved in a more gentlemanlike manner..." How those words have tortured me!*

*How could she have been so wrong about my character? How could she ever have believed Wickham? Did she have feelings for the scoundrel? How could she think that I persuaded Bingley purely because of an arrogant assumption?*

*And my letter! Did it make her think better of me? It must have, for why else would she have begged me for intelligence of Wickham? Why could I not suppress my anger and help her, without insisting on repayment? Now she must think me devoid of honour and integrity. She actually believed me capable of offering her the arrangement of a mistress, or of demanding that she do something immoral. How much lower can I sink in her opinion?*

*And now there is this situation here. We have spent a night together, on the same bed. I have seen and touched her body. I have truly compromised her. What can I do now but to offer for her again? And yet how can I be certain, if she accepts me, that it was not because she felt she had no other choice, but because she has genuine feelings for me?*

*And last night! The astonishing liberties that I took! Did I truly confess that I had fantasised her body from the very beginning of our acquaintance? Did I really pleasure her bosom? Oh, Lord! I feel sick.*

Thinking about her diminishing opinion of him, he could not bear lying next to her any longer. Instead, he left the bed and went in search of their clothes.

When he returned to the room, he changed back into his clothes quickly, then placed Elizabeth's clothes by the bed. He was just preparing to leave the room again when he heard her call out to him in a low voice.

"Good morning, Mr. Darcy."

Darcy was unwilling to turn to greet her. He whispered, "Good morning, Miss Bennet. I trust you slept well." His face turned red when he heard his own ill-chosen words. *How could she sleep well with you by her side, idiot?*

"Indeed, I slept well. Thank you. I…I may require your assistance…to dress."

Surprised by her request, he turned to look at her.

Elizabeth was sitting up on the bed, the sheet pulled up to cover her body. She was a vision of loveliness and enticement, though she still looked dishevelled and groggy from just awakening.

He looked away from the alluring picture she portrayed and murmured, "…To dress?"

"I fear I will need your assistance to…bind myself up."

"…bind up?" He asked.

"Yes."

"Oh!" Comprehension dawned on him. He glanced back at her, and at the cloth she held in her hand. "Of course," With trembling legs, he sat on the bed again.

She turned away from him, then let the bed sheet drop, presenting her smooth back to him. Then she started wrapping the cloth around her body from the front. When she pushed the cloth to the back under her right arm, she turned and asked him silently for assistance, with her eloquent eyes.

He moved closer, took the cloth and pulled it to her left until her hand touched his, near the underside of her left breast. Heat emitted from both their hands. He lowered his head, sorely tempted to kiss her shoulder.

She gasped, sensing his nearness.

Remembering her low opinion of him, especially after the previous night, he straightened immediately, but her forbidden proximity during the following few moments as he helped her to bind up her bosom were pure torture.

As soon as the task was completed, he left her alone to dress. Needing a breath of air in which to collect himself, he walked down to the beach, where he stood, skipping stones on the water.

Not long thereafter, he heard the sound of approaching footsteps and turned to see a little boy grinning at him. The boy had blond hair and a sweet face, reminding him of Georgiana when she was young.

"I luv ta t'row stones," the boy said.

"Yes, I love to throw stones, too," Darcy replied.

"Come! See crab." The boy, continuing to smile, ran toward him, took his hand and pulled him in the general direction of the hut. When they finally stopped at the end of the beach where the sand met the grass, the boy crouched down and pointed his finger eagerly at some moving crabs.

"Yes," Darcy agreed, "I can see a few crabs here."

"Why d'they walk sideways?" the boy asked, looking up at him.

Darcy sat down on the grass, watching them scuffle.

"Ye d' know?" the boy asked, and sat besides him.

"Well, a long time ago, crabs walked like you and I. But there was one shy crab who did not like to talk to strangers."

"Crabs ken talk?"

"Yes, they speak crab language, which we humans do not understand."

"What 'bout dat shy crab?"

"Well, one day, a dozen strange crabs set upon him, walking straight in front of him, asking him to dance with them. He was shy and wanted to avoid them, so he started walking sideways. Of course, the other crabs laughed and threw sand at him. Since then, he could only walk sideways."

"Dems 'twer bad crabs!"

"Ah, but one day, the shy crab came upon an injured crab stuck between two rocks. He helped her out and took her back to her home. When the injured crab asked him why he walked sideways, he did not explain but simply bid her goodbye."

"Din't da crab git bedder?"

"Yes, she got better and came to find him. They became good friends and she began to walk sideways, as he did. Do you know who she was?"

The boy shook his head zealously.

"She was the daughter of the King Crab."

"A princiss?!" " the boy exclaimed.

"Yes. And when the princess started to walk sideways, it became the fashion. Ever since then, everyone in the crab kingdom has been walking sideways too."

"I dunna like the princiss crab ! Girls trouble, like sister."

"Why do you not like her?"

" She bad. Pinch me."

Mr. Darcy smiled and ruffled his hair. "Why did she pinch you? Did you do something to annoy her?"

The boy shook his head fervently.

"Even if she is not nice, you still must take good care of her. She is your sister and she is a girl. We men have to take care of our girls and women."

"Papa say wemen's trouble!"

Darcy laughed out loud. "He jests. He loves your mother and your sister."

"I dunna luv girls. Dey's trouble!"

"You will love them when you grow older."

The boy wrinkled his nose and shook his head. "Yer older. De ye luv girls?"

"I do not love all girls. I love just two."

The conversation between the man and the boy was interrupted by the arrival of Margaret and Elizabeth. The latter was still dressed as a young boy, hat concealing her hair, and she leaned on her good foot. After a few pleasantries, the travellers bid the host and his family goodbye. Mr. Darcy took Elizabeth onto his back again and started up the hill.

Riding on his back, her hands around his neck, her legs around his waist, Elizabeth felt the warmth from his body heating up her chest. She had been standing near him and the boy for quite sometime, without them noticing it. She thought back to the story he had told the little boy, and his declaration of love, and her heart felt the warmth, as well. She laid her head onto his shoulder and breathed out a big sigh.

Mr. Darcy walked on silently. He could feel her soft body pressed against his back, her head on his shoulder, her breath tingling against his neck, and he wished he could carry her forever.

\*\*\*

After an hour of silent walking, they arrived near the inn at Whitstable. Mr. Darcy, finding his servants, asked them to bring a carriage around to meet him in the woods. When it arrived, he asked the servants to walk away for a few minutes. As soon as they had done so, he pulled down the shades over the windows so that he and Elizabeth could change into gentlemen's clothes inside the carriage. Then he went out to recall the servants and give instructions for the journey back to London.

On seeing the direction of the carriage, Elizabeth asked, "Are we not to search for Lydia?"

Darcy scowled. "I shall take you back to Gracechurch Street and return tomorrow."

"But you shall waste an entire day! Mr. Wickham and Lydia may disappear by then."

His lips thinned. "Madam, do not try my temper any more than you have already."

"Pray turn back the carriage. I can just as well wait for you at the inn. I promise not to follow you. I could not, anyway, with my injured foot."

"You know that you cannot remain with me without a chaperone."

"I am dressed as a gentleman right now. I do not see the problem. We have spent a night together already. What is one more? Please, I beg you, we must find Lydia without delay."

"You place no consequence upon the risk to your own reputation?"

"Mr. Darcy, it is not only men who wish to take good care of their family members."

Darcy blanched at her words, knowing that she had overheard what he said to the boy. Angry at her eavesdropping and her stubbornness, he glared at her. "If we turn back now, you shall become mine tonight!"

Before she could reply, the carriage jolted to a sudden halt.

## CHAPTER FOUR

Mr. Darcy looked out of the window and saw a mangled carriage in the roadway, blocking their passage. A young couple argued by its side.

Mr. Wickham and Miss Lydia!

Elizabeth heard her sister's voice, and was ready to stand up to bolt outside, but Darcy put a restraining hand on her shoulders and said sternly, "Stay here."

"But..."

"No. There is nothing to discuss. Do you truly want them to see you dressed in gentleman's clothes, riding with me inside a closed carriage without a chaperone? That would accomplish nothing but to give Wickham good excuse to demand yet more money."

Elizabeth bit her lower lip and sat down again as Mr. Darcy exited the carriage alone.

Waiting inside, she could not avoid thinking about his words, and about the scene that awaited him. *What has happened between Lydia and that scoundrel? Why are they arguing? And whatever did Mr. Darcy mean when he said that, if we turned back, I would become his tonight? Was it intended as a threat...or as a challenge? Would he truly take my innocence? I cannot help but wonder what it is like to be with a man – no, not 'a man,' but to be with him. He was so pleasant to the little boy on the beach. I have never seen that side of him. I believe he would be a wonderful father, telling fairy tales and stories to our children. Our children? Where did that thought come from? Lizzy! Do you have no shame?*

Elizabeth's thoughts went round and round in her head until, at last, Darcy came back to the carriage.

She asked immediately, "What happened? Is Lydia all right?"

"They are unharmed. They stayed in an inn in another village not far from here yesterday. It seems there was a disagreement with someone there, and they had to leave in a rush. Wickham drove recklessly and caused the carriage to turn over. He and Miss Lydia will take the second coach back to the next town. I have assigned a pair of burly servants to join them, to make certain that they do not escape again, and I brought the special licence I procured for them when I set off on this journey. Your uncle gave me the authority to have them marry in the nearest church, if I found them not to be married yet."

"Poor, stupid Lydia! To be forced to marry in haste, without family or friends attending, without even a decent dress, and to such a man!"

"It cannot be helped."

"Indeed it cannot. But may I not see to her, when we arrive in the next town, and attend the wedding?"

"Absolutely not! The fewer people who know of your presence here with me the better." His glare sharpened. "And it has just come to my mind to wonder how you persuaded my head coachman to let you pretend to be a footman. Did Georgiana aid you?"

Elizabeth hesitated for a moment, then nodded her head, "I told Georgiana you might call Mr. Wickham out, and that we had to prevent it."

"Why would she think that you could prevent me from doing so? Your acquaintance with her is still very new, and she is not very trusting to strangers." Darcy stared at her, challenging her to tell the truth.

"I told her…" Elizabeth breathed deeply, looked down at her nervously clasped hands, and confessed, "I told her that you and I had been secretly engaged since your visit to Rosings, when I was visiting Charlotte." She returned his gaze, daring him to vent his anger at her deception.

"Is that so?" He could scarcely believe it but he contented himself with simply nodding his head as he wondered, *Is her opinion of me truly so changed that she would be willing to follow through on a secret engagement between us?* "And what of your aunt?" he asked. "What did you tell her about your absence?"

"I told her that I would be staying with Georgiana, because you needed to search for the wayward pair but your sister's companion had been called away suddenly."

"Very creative!" he observed dryly.

"Desperate times call for desperate measures. I truly *was* afraid that you would call Wickham out."

"Why would you worry? I am far more proficient than he with both sword and pistol."

"That may well be, but I would not want you harmed in any way."

Darcy's somber mood lifted on hearing her worries about him. However, he wanted to make certain of her stand. "Or is it that you would not want me harming him?"

"That, too."

His countenance again turned grim. He took a deep breath and asked the inevitable question. "Tell me, did you follow me in order to prevent Wickham's marriage to your sister?"

"Prevent? What are you talking about?"

"You said you were pleased with the preference of Mr. Wickham. Perhaps you want him for yourself."

"Are you out of your mind? That was before I knew of his character. Did I not say yesterday that we must have him marry Lydia and send them off to one of the colonies?"

"Then…uhm…You are not in love with him?"

"Never!"

"But you said you would not want me to harm him."

"Of course not! What if you were sent to prison for life or faced the gallows for murdering him? I could not bear to see *any* sort of harm come to you!"

The burden in Darcy's mind was lifted. He wanted to ask her whether her opinion of him had changed so much that she would now be willing to accept his suit…but he did not dare.

He closed his eyes and simply savoured the knowledge that she was, at least, not in love with Wickham, and that she cared for him enough not to want him to face any dangers. *She does not want me to be harmed. She cares about me! She has told Georgiana that we are engaged. Her aunt and uncle know of my interest in her. There is still hope that I may win her heart.*

Elizabeth did not understand why he had closed his eyes and stopped talking altogether. She looked at him, and saw the throbbing of a vein on his forehead. He looked weary. She longed to move across and smooth his frowning brow…but she did not dare.

*He is still so young, and already he shoulders so many responsibilities. He shows a sense of determination and decisiveness that is not present in Mr. Bingley. Just look at the number of people who work for him in his townhouse. As a brother, a landlord, a master, he could bestow much pleasure or pain. He could have done much good or evil. And yet, when I sat next to the coachmen and listened to their conversations, they were a content and sensible lot, much happier than the servants at Netherfield, under Mr. or Miss Bingley's patronage.*

*Although the coachmen did not commend their master in front of me, their levelheaded and cheerful outlook on life speaks volumes about their sense of loyalty in serving the Darcy family, and about the character of the master himself.*

She stared at the exhausted man. She thought of his love with a deeper sentiment of gratitude than she had ever felt before; she remembered his gentlemanly ways, his warmth, and the caring manner that softened the stiff, reserved way in which he had expressed himself in times past. She was thankful for the strength of his love, a love which defied his own will, persisting against his reason and perhaps even against his character. She was grateful to him, not merely for having once loved her, but for loving her still.

She remembered his word to the little boy on the beach. He did not love any one but Georgiana…and herself. *Am I too fickle to respect and esteem a man whom I professed to dislike so much, just a few days ago? I am certain he demanded a reward to taunt or goad me, for saying he was not behaving in a gentlemanlike manner during his proposal at Hunsford. Now I know that he is a truly honourable man.* On this reassuring thought, she followed his example and closed her eyes to rest.

***

When the coaches arrived in Herne Bay, Elizabeth heard Mr. Darcy instruct his coachmen to take Wickham and Lydia directly to St. Martin Church. He then settled her into a room at the New Dolphin Inn, and followed after them.

She expected him, in company with the Wickhams, to return within an hour, but the hour turned into two. She was tugging nervously at her hair, pacing back and forth, when someone finally knocked upon her door. Opening it, she found Darcy's head coachman, Wharton, standing there. He hurriedly asked her to take care of his master in the adjacent room for the time being.

Elizabeth did not understand his request, but he was gone before she could utter a word. She ran to the room and found Mr. Darcy lying on the bed, with bandaged wounds on his head and his chest, as still as…

Fearing the worst, she ran to him, but closer inspection showed that, although his eyes were closed, he was still breathing.

"Mr. Darcy, what happened? How were you injured? Where are Lydia and Mr. Wickham?" She shook his shoulder lightly.

Darcy opened his eyes and looked at her, barely able to speak. "Elizabeth, forgive me. I am truly sorry. They are gone."

"Gone? You mean they have escaped again?"

He shook his head, then groaned in pain.

The sound spurred Elizabeth to action. She summoned warm water and food from a servant. Then she helped him eat a little, but he only wanted some water to drink. She proceeded to gently wash away the bloodstains on his head and chest. One of the bandages was already soaking through. He needed a doctor!

Her eyes widened with the sudden terrible memory of his words...*Gone*? The blood on his head and his chest. Could they...Had he...

She had to know at once. "Mr. Darcy, do you mean to say that they are both...dead?"

Sadly, he nodded his head.

Had their earlier conversation become a reality? She could not...would not accept that he might be responsible for murder and possibly be sent to prison. In a trembling voice, she asked, "Who...who killed them?"

"Mrs. Younge's sister."

Elizabeth released a big sigh, relieved that Darcy had not been the one. "But why?"

"It seems that Wickham had previously seduced the woman, before he went to Hertfordshire, and that he had promised to marry her when he returned. He did not keep in touch with her. But yesterday when he was in the neighbourhood, she happened upon him. They had an argument when she saw your sister with him. That was why Wickham and Miss Lydia fled. She then followed us to the church, but she arrived after the ceremony had finished. She attacked and killed him when we were walking out of the church. My burly servants were not there and I was not quick enough to stop her. Your sister jumped ahead to struggle with the assailant. I am so sorry, but…she was killed during the struggle."

"Oh, Lord!" As the news of Lydia's death finally sank in, Elizabeth sat down next to him, speechless, with tears streaming down her face. She could not believe that Lydia, so young, so full of life and laughter, could be gone in the blink of an eye. How very tragic to be married one minute and then to meet her judgment immediately afterwards. "Oh dear, what will Mama and Papa say? They shall be heart-broken."

Mr. Darcy held her hands, barely able to respond again. He patiently waited, desperately wanting to comfort her in his arms. When she finally composed herself, he whispered, "Elizabeth, I am so very sorry. I should have acted faster and held your sister back."

Elizabeth shook her head. She was certain that he had done the best he could. Before she could reply to him, however, the doctor arrived to tend to his wounds. She left them together and waited in the hallway, only to hear Mr. Darcy groaning in pain.

She decided to seek out Wharton and ask him to recount how his master had been injured. The man replied that Mr. Darcy had tried to shield the newly wed from the mad woman, and was injured in the process. Afterwards, he had succeeded in subduing the woman. Wharton had helped him hastily bandage up his wounds, and they then saw to the care of the couples' bodies and reported the killings to the authorities. The coachman explained to Elizabeth that his master had insisted on taking care of everything else first, when he should have immediately been attended to by a doctor.

After the doctor finished treating Darcy's wounds, he informed Elizabeth that Mr. Darcy had lost a great deal of blood, but that he was a strong man and  was not in any life-threatening danger. However, he asked Elizabeth to keep an eye on the patient throughout the night, in case he developed a fever. In addition, the doctor told her how to clean and re-dress Darcy's wounds to prevent infection.

That night, Elizabeth stayed with him as he became somewhat delirious from fever. He tossed and turned violently, murmuring incoherently of his childhood escapades with Mr. Wickham. Elizabeth wiped the sweat from his face, neck and chest throughout the night, keeping cool cloths on his head to help reduce his fever. At one time, when his sleep seemed most disturbed, she sat down on the bed and pulled him over her lap, massaging his head and shoulders. Her calm ministering manner seemed to settle him. Only when he was peaceful again did Elizabeth feel that she could stretch out next to him, to rest a little herself.

*** 

The next morning, Mr. Darcy woke to find Elizabeth on the bed with him once again, only this time she was dressed in gentlemen's clothing. His head had rested again on her bosom as his pillow and, in spite of the pain he felt in other parts of his body, his heart was quite contented by her embrace. Then, abruptly, he remembered the terrible events of the previous day. Wickham, dead! He had been a scoundrel, and had deserved punishment for his deeds, but surely nothing as severe as to meet such a violent death.

*If only George had taken the opportunities offered to him by my father to improve his situation through education, his life could have been totally different. Then Mrs. Younge's sister, mad! Love can indeed make or break a person. Is this a premonition of what could happen as a result of my passionate love for Elizabeth? Should I let her go? Miss Lydia, to die so young. It is all very tragic. She was just of Georgiana's age, and should have had so much life before her. I wonder whether Elizabeth feels that I have failed her. What more could I have possibly done to prevent this tragedy from happening? And yet how untenable is seems to be so powerless in the face of events.*

He pulled his aching body up, waking Elizabeth in the process. They greeted each other with embarrassment and sadness. She wanted him to rest for another day before leaving for London but he was determined to lose no more time. He told her he was feeling fine.

Mr. Darcy remained silent throughout the journey back to London. His body ached, and his thoughts were in turmoil. *The Gardiners will surely be worried about Elizabeth, and I do not wish her reputation to be more ruined if this compromising adventure with me should ever be made public. I love her too much to allow any further damage to occur, if I can possibly prevent it.*

*We must return as soon as possible to London. But should I ask for her hand again now? Would she accept me, after what I allowed to happen to cause the death of her sister? She must hate me now. I do not know what action to take. I am too weary to deal with this right now. All that I know to do is to return her to the safety of her family, and to inform them of the unfortunate details of what has befallen Lydia and Wickham. For now, I dare do no more.*

\*\*\*

Depending upon circumstance, six months could be either a long or a very short time. For Elizabeth, the six months spent in mourning were extremely long. She had not seen Mr. Darcy since they parted at Gracechurch Street. His last parting gaze at her was imbedded in her memory, grim and disheartening. He had made all of the arrangements necessary for her to leave London, and had further taken care of the transportation of the bodies of Miss Lydia and her brief, yet legal husband Mr. Wickham. All had arrived safely back at Longbourn in the comforts provided by Darcy's carriages. He had sent Elizabeth home with her sickly father and his man servant, with the addition of a maid to accompany her.

But since that day, a long six months ago, she had received no communication from Mr. Darcy or his sister. She no longer knew what he thought of her, or whether she would ever see him again.

Life at Longbourn was bleak and depressing. Mrs. Bennet, hysterical, was inconsolable upon learning of the violent death of her younger daughter, so soon after the marriage. She blamed Colonel Forster for not taking care of Lydia properly in Brighton, blamed Mr. Wickham for seducing the mad woman, blamed the Gardiners and Elizabeth for allowing Lydia to run away a second time, and blamed her poor husband for not finding the pair sooner. She stayed in her room most of the time, still blaming everyone but herself, and demanding constant attention from her daughters and servants.

The only happy news was that Mr. Bennet had recovered, not long after their return from London, and seemed not to suffer any major damage from the strain to his heart, beyond a slight limp in his right leg. It was a tremendous relief since, had he, too, met his judgment, they would surely all have been displaced from Longbourn, and Elizabeth thought privately that her mother might well have gone mad, if that turn of events had occurred.

On the day that the Bennets packed up their mourning clothes, Mrs. Bennet received the best news from her sister,

Mrs. Philips: Mr. Bingley would be returning to Netherfield, the following week.

Elizabeth's heart-beat skipped on hearing the news. *Is he coming to see me?* Of course, she was not thinking of Mr. Bingley, but of his friend, Mr. Darcy. After two weeks of endless waiting, finally a horse was heard one morning approaching Longbourn. It was Mr. Bingley...but, to her extreme disappointment, he arrived for a visit alone. She fought back tears at having her expectations raised only to be brought back crashing down again in such disappointment. If she had not been so curious to gain some intelligence about his friend, Elizabeth would have fled the room to privately express her distress. Instead, she composed herself, determined to support her sister, Jane, through this first meeting with Mr. Bingley.

In the event, Mr. Bingley stayed for tea but declined dinner. He tried repeatedly to engage Miss Bennet in conversation, but Jane was even more quiet than usual. Mrs. Bennet managed to monopolise the conversation, thus inadvertently helping the couple to overcome the awkwardness of their first meeting after such a long separation.

When he was ready to leave, Mr. Bingley addressed Elizabeth, handing her a letter...from Miss Darcy. He had almost forgotten his message, so distracted was he at seeing his angel, Jane, again. He finally told Elizabeth that she was invited by Miss Darcy to visit Pemberley as soon as Elizabeth could find the time. He further added that Georgiana and her brother were both eager to renew their acquaintance since they last met in London.

Elizabeth's hands trembled when she held the letter. Her countenance turned from desperation to hope. *He has not forgotten me! He has sent for me - finally!*

# CHAPTER FIVE

Pemberley in late October was magnificent. The weather was getting colder, even in sunlight, but the Buxwood, Yew and multi-coloured fallen leaves created a vibrant mosaic that framed the great estate.

Elizabeth drew a deep breath of the crisp morning air as she walked to the maze.

She had been crestfallen, the previous evening, to have found only Georgiana waiting to welcome their party when Elizabeth and Mr. and Mrs. Gardiner arrived. It seemed that a tenant problem on the far west side of the estate's property had called Mr. Darcy away. But the young girl reassured her that he was looking forward to seeing them all again, and Georgiana welcomed Elizabeth like a long lost sister. They did not talk much during dinner, as Georgiana was not used to playing hostess and Elizabeth's heart was heavy with anticipation and disappointment. They all retired early from an exhausting day of travel.

Elizabeth tossed and turned the whole night. Although she had been placed in the most comfortable and luxuriant bedchamber in which she had ever stayed, she found herself longing to embrace Mr. Darcy to her bosom, wanting nothing more than to be transported back to the hours they had spent together at that fisherman's hut where they had, at least and at last, been quite alone together.

She woke up very early and walked out along the garden path, where finally she came upon the maze, at the most remote part of the garden. Its tall bushes were trimmed and shaped most intriguingly, and she walked into it, her heart full of thoughts of the owner of the great estate. While her gaze traversed flowers, pots, and statues along the many twists and turns, her thoughts reflected upon her life, reviewing the things she had done and discussed with this man.

After half an hour in the maze, she decided to return to the house, but when she turned round, she soon discovered that she was lost, unable to find her way out. It seemed a wryly apt reflection of her life. Was she never to find a way out of the confusing situations into which she got herself? Would Mr. Darcy finally decide that his love for her was over? Would his ardent admiration fade away, just when she had at last found her love for him?

She could not bear to face such a possibility. She must find a way for him to love her as he once had. She must.

So decided, she ran from one lane to another, feeling more and more like a trapped animal in a cage. Soon, in her rush to find the way out, she twisted her recently injured ankle, which only made her remember how Mr. Darcy had carried her, a recollection that added to her state of melancholy. She berated herself for having fallen into such a panic as to hurt herself once again. Leaning gingerly against the bushes for support, she took a deep breath, commanding herself to calmness.

Soon, although the thought pleased her not at all, she decided that she would have to call out for assistance while she slowly, painfully continued her search for the exit.

"Help! Someone please help me! I am lost in this maze! Help!" Elizabeth yelled as she limped along the twisting paths, hoping that one of the gardeners might hear her.

Suddenly she heard her name. "Elizabeth! Where are you?"

The echoing voice of Mr. Darcy was sweet balm on her wounded soul. She limped toward the sound of his voice, turning around another set of bushes. "Mr. Darcy," she called with renewed hope, "I am here."

"Elizabeth!" Finally, Mr. Darcy came to her vision. He looked thinner than when she had seen him last, with an air of distress and exhaustion. "Elizabeth, my lord! What happened to you?" He walked straight to her and wrapped his arms around her waist, taking much of the weight from her injured ankle.

"Mr. Darcy, you are finally here!" She was overcome with emotion. The grief of the past six months, the uncertainty of not knowing whether she would see him again, the crazed worry of feeling forever trapped in the maze, all combined to overtake her. She rose on her tiptoes, wrapped her arms around his neck, pressed her face to his shoulder and began to cry.

\*\*\*

Mr. Darcy, for his part, was still not completely recovered from the infected wound he had suffered. Added to his concerns, the emotional trauma of witnessing Wickham's violent death and the gloomy sense of unrequited love from not knowing whether Elizabeth would forgive him had proven nearly too much for him to bear, through these long, lonely months of uncertainty. Indeed, at one time, he had wished to rest his body and mind forever.

His sister had begged him to send word of his continued illness to Elizabeth, but he would have none of that. He could not bear to worry her when she was in mourning, and while her father was still sick. What constructive purpose could it serve to reveal to her that he, himself, was ill? She would not have been free to come to visit him, even if she desired to do so. It would have only added to her burden. He loved her too much to let her worry about him.

In the end, he tried to stay resolved to the hope that she did not want him to be harmed.

In the months that followed, his body slowly recovered, but his spirits were still uncertain. Once he was physically strong enough, he sought out Bingley, to correct his officious interference concerning Miss Bennet. Then he returned to Pemberley, determined to prepare for Elizabeth's arrival.

When six months had passed, a proper and respectful time period for those in mourning, he at last felt free to instruct Georgiana to extend an invitation to the Gardiners and Elizabeth, as originally planned. Moreover, Mr. Bingley was due to return to Netherfield, and Mr. Darcy knew that he would be doing a friend a service by asking him to deliver the message.

In the event, Mr. Darcy was deeply frustrated not to be available to welcome Elizabeth to Pemberley on the day of her arrival. But even the best-laid plans could be derailed by unexpected events. In this case, a pressing tenant problem called him away, and he was not even able to be there when she spent the first night in his home. Thus he was robbed of witnessing her first impression when she viewed Pemberley. Did she approve of it? Her good opinion was so rarely bestowed that it would have been a wonder to see her fine eyes brighten when she first arrived.

When he had finally ridden back to Pemberley this morning, he felt done in and frustrated. He came expecting to have a short rest before meeting the love of his life in pristine gentleman's clothing and a calm and steady manner. But, purely by chance, he had walked past the maze and had heard her cry for help. His mind wheeled with worry. What had happened? Surely she could not come to any harm within the sanctuary of his home. He could not allow that to happen, now that they were to see each other again. Dismounting hastily, he rushed into the maze, only to be confronted by the sight of a distressed and limping Elizabeth.

In that moment, he paid no mind to propriety. He called Elizabeth by her Christian name and wrapped his arms around her tiny waist, determined to take the weight from her injured leg. Even then, however, he had not anticipated that she would so far forget herself as to wrap her dear arms around his neck. Nor was he prepared for her tears, which made his heart ache.

Overcome, he picked her up and walked a short distance to where a bench stood, at one of the turns in the maze. He settled her on his lap, still tightly embracing her as he rocked her, murmured comforting words for her ears only.

After several minutes, Elizabeth was finally able to stop sobbing. Without regard to manner, she pulled his coat up to wipe her eyes. He silently found his handkerchief and placed it in her hand to dry her tears.

Elizabeth felt as if she had needed those healing tears to release the suffering and grief of the last six months. Her spirit returned, fed by the knowledge that Mr. Darcy was embracing and comforting her in this moment of distress. But then she remembered his non-communication for the worst months of her life. She pouted, pushed herself away from him, and looked him squarely in the eyes. "Why did you not try to contact me, these past six months?"

Mr. Darcy looked at her and replied, "I am afraid I was quite ill for a time."

"What! You were sick and did not tell me of it?"

"What good could that have done? I could not send for you. You were in mourning. I knew that your father was also ill and still had need of you."

"What illness befell you?"

"Not an illness, precisely. My wounds became infected. I was feverish for quite a while, and very weak after that. It took me a long while to regain my strength."

Elizabeth gasped, distraught that she had not been there to nurse him. "What if you had not recovered!" she exclaimed, horrified by the thought.

He winced at the volume of her words.

Seeing his expression, she traced his lean cheeks with her fingertips and said, in a much softer voice, "No wonder you look so thin and tired! And you had tenant problems, last night. Have you slept at all?"

Wearily, he shook his head.

"But that cannot be borne!" she protested in concern. "How can you not look after yourself? You have only recently recovered. We must get you inside, out of the cold." She rose from his lap and took a limping step, but he stopped her with a touch.

"Elizabeth, I am fine. Truly. I have not felt so well in quite some time. Right now, I want nothing more than to hold you for a little longer. As soon as we return to the house, I will have to pretend to be a gentleman, and sit as far from you as possible, when all I really want is to take you upon my lap and keep holding you." He drew her down again and held her tightly, then said in an irritated tone, "And who are you to be taking such a tone with me? You have not taken proper care of yourself, either. I can see that you have hurt your ankle again. Am I to carry you around forever?"

"I...I...got lost, here in the maze, and I felt trapped, like an animal in a cage. It was altogether too much like what I have been feeling for the past six months, tormenting myself over whether you still love me." She looked up at him, her expression a peculiar blend of daring and entreaty. "Can you possibly still want me, after what happened to Lydia and Mr. Wickham?"

He frowned pensively. "I might well ask the same of you."

She inhaled deeply, determined to bare her soul to him. "I...admire your courage in righting the wrong. I respect your character, which makes you such a responsible master. I think highly of your love for Georgiana. I most definitely do not want you to be harmed in any way. I want to take care of you when you are well, when you are drunk, when you are ill." She lowered her head before whispering to him, "I...I love you! Indeed I do."

She held her breath, waiting for him to reply, and saw that, although he closed his eyes for a moment, his frown did not ease. Then he opened his eyes and asked slowly, again, "You do not blame me for your sister's downfall?"

"How could I blame you? I know that you did all that you could do to save my sister. I believe the Bible when it tells us, 'As ye sow, so shall ye reap.' As painful a truth as it may be, Lydia was responsible for her own demise."

He embraced her again, then pushing her far enough away so that he could see her eyes. "And...you...love me enough to...be willing to be...my mistress?"

Elizabeth's eyes widened. *Does he mean to threaten or challenge me?* She looked at him directly. He seemed to be scorched by her intense gaze and turned his head slightly away.

She replied calmly, "Love is all about making the other person happy. If by becoming your mistress, it will make you happy, I shall do it." She lowered her mouth to kiss him softly before asking, "And so, do you still love me?"

He wanted to cling to her pleasing lips but he could not pretend anymore; whatever the risk, he felt that he must be honest with her or die. "Oh, Elizabeth! I loved you in the past, I love you now, and I will always love you! My wish is to make you the happiest woman in the world. I would never demean you by expecting you to be my mistress. I have never thought of asking you as my mistress, except as the mistress of Pemberley itself. Pray forgive me for testing you, when we first met again in London. Pray forgive me for challenging you again, just now. My self-confidence and my pride were painfully bruised by your refusal in Kent. I needed to be certain before I asked for your hand again. Elizabeth, dearest Elizabeth, will you do me the honour of becoming my wife?"

Tears welled in her eyes again. She said decisively, "Yes, Fitzwilliam. I have hoped and waited for you to renew your proposal, for some months now. I love you most fervently and it shall be my honour to become your wife."

Her reply awoke a flame of joy within him. He wrapped his arms tightly around her body and bestowed upon her a tender kiss, one which lingered and grew more passionate.

Finally, when they released each other in order to catch their breath, Elizabeth urged him to head back. She did not want him to stay in the cold air for long, and she had been out from the house for some time as well. She feared that her aunt and uncle would be worried for her.

Like any young man violently in love, Mr. Darcy was in a jubilant mood. He could not wipe the smile from his face or the passionate glint from his eyes. In truth, he did not want to share her with anyone else, just yet. He wanted to stay here alone with her forever. But that, of course, could not be.

He suddenly remembered some of his happy days here in the maze with his cousin, Colonel Fitzwilliam. Even now, he could not imagine how Richard had become a successful soldier for his cousin had the worst sense of direction. As a boy, he had often gotten lost in the maze. Mr. Darcy, as any carefree young lad would do, would take advantage of the situation and extract toys and promises from him, in return for revealing the way out. Remembering the mischief on his younger days, he flashed a devilish grin and told his new fiancée, "Well then, what reward do you offer me for leading you out of this maze?"

The mention of a reward reminded her of an earlier bargain they had made, but Elizabeth loved his change of countenance, which made him appear wonderfully younger and more relaxed. Resolutely, she decided to forget the sad past and play along with his teasing. Raised her eyebrows archly, she stated, "I did not know that you had gone into trade. Still, with an injured ankle, I am at your mercy here, Sir! Pray, name your price."

"Very well. I want…an article of your clothing for each turn out of the maze."

"Scandalous! That is most ungentlemanly of you. Besides, what will the gardeners say when they find their future mistress, less formally attired than is her custom, emerging from the maze in the arms of their master? And may I remind you that we are outside in the cold autumn weather? What if I should catch a cold?"

"Gardeners be damned! They had better get used to it, for I intend to explore every maze, bush and pond on Pemberley's grounds with my wife, come summer. And if you catch a cold, I will lie in bed with you, to warm your whole body...and your heart."

Elizabeth's face turned bright red, thinking back to their two nights together, but she would not allow him to win the argument so easily. "You are determined to keep my articles of clothing as souvenirs? Tell me, how many turns are there before we get out of this bothersome maze? And how would I know you do not detour on purpose? I do not have all that many articles of clothing upon me, today. No, I think we need to discuss another form of reward, lest we scandalise the whole of Pemberley."

Darcy swallowed, thinking about stripping her of all of the items that she wore, one by one. He remembered her gorgeous, naked bosom. How he wished the weather were warmer, and that they were alone in some secluded Eden. But he conceded the reality of their present situation, and so his thoughts whirled until he came up with another, equally satisfying bargain to present to his beloved.

"Well, it is tiring to carry you around. I deserve to be handsomely rewarded for sustaining such a heavy task. How about ... a kiss for every turn of the maze?"

"Me, heavy! Never!" Elizabeth smacked him lightly on the shoulder. Then she looked at him bravely and said, "But how difficult can a kiss be? Hmmm? I believe, Sir, that we have struck a bargain."

He lowered his mouth immediately, ready to reap his reward, but he did not kiss her mouth. Instead, he licked and bit her neck, just where it met her shoulder.

She gasped and protested, "You said a kiss, sir!"

Darcy grinned. "I did not specify your lips alone. There are many places on your body which I wish and dare to kiss. And I plan to teach you where each and every one of them is, during the coming days and years we will have together, my dearest, loveliest Elizabeth." His intense declaration caused Elizabeth's body to flush with heat. He carried her in his arms and walked purposely along the next track before turning right, then stopped, ready to claim his second kiss. "Uhm, where shall I kiss you, this time?"

Elizabeth's body trembled with anticipation. "My eyes, sir?"

"Oh, a kiss for two locations? It bodes well that you are so generous, my love."

He lowered his head but, rather than bestowing kisses upon her eyes, he kissed each of her breasts, through the fabric of the thick spencer.

Elizabeth felt as if her heart were jumping out of her chest. She could feel the warmth from his mouth stimulating her nipples, promising future pleasures. Then, after what seemed like endless minutes, he raised his head and walked on. Only then did she object breathlessly, "You are not doing what you said!"

"When did I say I would kiss your eyes?"

"Oh, Fitzwilliam, you delight in vexing me!"

"You are starting to talk like your mother already. I was hoping you would not do that until you reached the grand old age of fifty."

"Those are the most unkind words you have uttered in our acquaintance! Heartless man, to compare me with Mama."

They bantered and exchanged hot, sensual kisses until they emerged from the maze. Engrossed in one another, the happy couple entered the house via the side entrance, never once stopping to wonder whether their intimate moments were being observed by a pair of disapproving eyes.

# CHAPTER SIX

Mr. Darcy took a soothing sip of port, then rested his head on the settee in his bedroom.

This, he thought with satisfaction, was a tremendously important day. His second proposal had met with success. Finally, he had won the heart of his beloved. He felt wonderful, not feel tired at all, and he wanted to savor every remaining moment of the day.

The return of Mr. Darcy with his new fiancée in his arm to the house had been met with an array of raised eyebrows and loud exclamations. After explaining about Elizabeth's injured ankle, the couple had retired to their separate bedchambers for some rest.

It transpired that Elizabeth's ankle was not seriously hurt, and she was able to walk almost normally soon afterwards after being tended to by the doctor. They spent the afternoon and dinner in a pleasant manner. He was not a man of many words in front of people. His thoughts were focused on the scorching kisses that he and Elizabeth had shared in the maze. His eyes were filled with phantom visions of Elizabeth, bedecked in simple, elegant dresses, gracing the rooms of

Pemberley. In the present moment, he was quite content to simply rest his gaze upon Elizabeth, thinking all manner of pleasant thoughts about her and about their future together.

The only sour turn of the day was the unexpected intrusion, before dinner, of Mr. and Mrs. Hurst and Miss Bingley. The travellers said they were on their way to visit friends in the next county, but that their carriage had broken down not far from Pemberley. Mr. Darcy had no decent choice but to offer to host them for a day or two, until their carriage could be repaired.

Miss Bingley was exceptionally polite to his invited guests, which he thought a bit strange, as she had previously been most uncivil to Elizabeth. He was also suspicious of their arrival. It was too much of a coincidence. But he would not allow them to distract him from his pleasure.

He had even taken the time, before preparing to retire, to visit the connecting bedroom. He unlocked all the doors, drew aside the curtain and looked around the mistress's room. He opened the cupboards and drawers, and imagined visiting Elizabeth there when she was finally his wife. It was a happy thought indeed.

Now, as the day drew to a close, Mr. Darcy took another sip of the port and turned his mind to their future, then started, his eyes widening with surprise, as he saw the connecting door to the mistress' bedchamber begin to open.

***

She had bent her wits to listening to the servants and questioning Miss Darcy in the most cunning way, both before and after dinner, determined to carry out her plan: she wanted Mr. Darcy to be hers tonight, not a moment later.

Having obtained the necessary intelligence about his routine, she found it rather easy to find her way, and was relieved not to have to go to him via the servant's entrance, for she found that the door of the mistress's room was not locked. The curtain was drawn aside, granting her a glimpse of the interior. A dreamy smile spread on her face. Walking to the connecting door, she turned the knob and slowly pushed open the door, where Mr. Darcy looked gratifyingly astonished by her visit.

"Elizabeth! What are you doing here?" He sat up quickly, nearly spilling the port from his glass

Elizabeth locked the door behind her and stopped there, gazing at him. She was wearing a simple day dress in yellow, but the décolleté was daring. Her breathing was quick and shallow, from the adventure of seeking him out, and from seeing him without his coat and cravat. His shirt gapped open, allowing her a glimpse of his virile chest. He was still in his tight breeches, resting comfortably on the settee by the fire, with legs apart. She could not help but stall a glance at his bulge, although she diverted her gaze away immediately from the impressive sight.

Softly, she whispered, "Fitzwilliam, make me yours."

She saw him frown, as if he had not heard – or did not understand – what she had just said. The room was nearly silent for a moment, with only the crackle of the fire as counterpoint to their heavy breathing.

Mr. Darcy put the glass down, then stood, and walked slowly over to her. Placing his hands lightly on her shoulders, he asked softly, "Elizabeth, have you thought clearly about this?"

She shivered from the potent contact of his touch. He was too tall, too big. Shaken, she took his hand and led him back to the settee, pushing him to sit down again. Standing in front of him, she took a deep breath and said, "I have been thinking about this for months. One can be so full of life and laughter one minute…and then, unexpectedly, one be gone, in the blink of an eye. Fitzwilliam, I love you. I want to be with you. Even if you had not proposed to me, this morning. Even if you had not offered me any position in your life. I have been determined about this for quite a long time. I want to be yours. Now."

Mr. Darcy inhaled, breathing in her sweet lavender scent, then closed his eyes, overwhelmed by a multitude of emotions. He could scarcely believe what he had just heard. *She has loved me all these past months. She loves me enough to abandon propriety and her reputation. She was even willing to be mine without the offer of marriage or any other proper arrangement to protect herself.*

"Fitzwilliam? Are you unwell? Did you…? Do you not want me?"

The uncertainty in her voice aroused him from his thoughts. Opened his eyes, he pulled her onto his lap and embraced her, then released her just as suddenly, gazing deeply into her eyes. "Do I not want you? My dearest Elizabeth, I have wanted you for so very long that I can scarcely believe my good fortune. Nothing will please me more than to be united with you, joining our bodies and souls together. We are already betrothed, as far as I am concerned. It shall not be long before we are truly husband and wife."

"But I want to be yours now."

He heard her reply, yet he was still unsure what to do, as he struggled between remaining a gentleman or abandoning all principles by seizing the moment.

"Your father…" He started to say. But when she slipped her hands inside his opened shirt and caressed his chest, he was lost completely. Her tentative fingers were burning matches that torched his body, searing him not with pain but with passion and pleasure.

He enfolded her body again and kissed her with all the pent-up ardour of the past year. Ravenous, he wetted her lips and teased her mouth open with his tongue, thrusting inside her syrupy entrance to trace her inner muscles and duel with her soft tongue. Unable to resist, he sucked at it, drawing her tongue into his mouth.

His hands traced her daring neckline. When his knuckles grazed her soft flesh, he felt her shiver with desire. After a few long minutes of petting and caressing every inch of exposed flesh that he could reach, he unbuttoned her dress and eased it off her shoulders. She, in turn, helped him with it impatiently, baring her bosom for his exploration.

At that, he stopped his kisses and pushed her slightly away from him. His gaze focused on her gorgeous breasts, drinking in the deep red aureoles. He found that he accurately remembered every curve of her body from their previous encounters. Lowering his mouth, he surrendered to his need, licking and kissing her bosom with an intensity that seemed to make her lose all coherent thought as well, as his lips suckled her breast. He drew a nipple into his mouth, brushing it with his teeth, and heard her gasp with delight. Then he used his tongue to twirl around it, wetting, lapping, tasting her.

Meanwhile, his hands were busy with other parts of her body. His left hand cupped her other breast while he gently pinched its nipple; at the same time, with a daring that left him light-headed, the fingers of his right hand stroked her inner thighs. He was painfully aroused, his straining manhood heated against her bottom, making her squirm on his lap.

It was too much for him. He pushed her to stand up and pulled the dress further down. It dropped to the floor and pooled around her feet. He devoured her naked upper body with his eyes before lowering them to take in her alluring undergarment, which still concealed her treasure from his prying eyes.

Driven by need, he stood up as well, swept her up, carried her the few necessary steps, then gently placed her on his bed. Elizabeth, on his bed. His senses reeled.

She did not cover her body but lay there, her glittering, fine eyes looking up at him trustingly. Urgently, he stripped off his shirt and pushed down the confining fabric of his breeches.

Elizabeth's eyes widened at the sight of his muscular, nude body, and he saw her swallow hard, for the first time since entering his rooms. She did not seem to be afraid of him, and she made no attempt to rise, but he could see her apprehension at viewing his naked manhood in its present magnified state.

He lay down by her side, gently pushing a few strands of her dishevelled hair away from her face. "Dearest Elizabeth," he murmured, kissing her forehead and then the tip of her nose. "Tell what you are thinking."

She swallowed again before replying, "You are so… magnificent. I am worried…I do not know how…Fitzwilliam, I am concerned that I will not be able to satisfy you."

"Elizabeth, my love, I know you are an innocent maiden. This is not just about me being satisfied. It is about you having pleasure as well." He lowered his mouth and kissed her soft lips. "Trust me, my love. Let me show you. "

When she nodded her consent, he began in earnest, restraining his ardour and exploring her body with tenderness. When he smoothed her undergarment and stockings away, his kisses followed his hands, tracing lower and lower.

Elizabeth thrashed and arched her body.

When he parted her legs and bestowed kiss after kiss on her secret Eden, her moans became louder and more uninhibited, as if she were purely a creature of the senses, no longer able to think, only feel. Mr. Darcy continued to ravish her body, wooing the hot lava from deep within her. When she reached the peak of her pleasure, she actually screamed aloud, clearly overcome.

At that signal, he quickly raised his body and lodged his raging manhood against her wet entrance, pressing into her with slow insistence. She was extremely tight, but the abundance of her body's natural moisture allowed him a smooth entry into her inner core. His thick shaft delved slowly upward until he reached her virginal barrier. At that, he stopped his movements, but only for a moment, as he gazed down at her flushed face. Then, braced on knees and elbows, he returned his hands to her twin peaks, pinching and pleasuring the peaked nipples while he pressed his tongue into her mouth. After a few minutes invested in arousing her again, he felt her body stir beneath him with returning excitement. At that, he braced himself and thrust strongly into her. The sensation that rewarded this effort left him barely coherent, caught up in a rush of intense pleasure as the obstruction yielded, enabling him to become deeply engulfed within her. His final clear thought was, *she is mine, finally and completely mine!*

Elizabeth cried out in pain but he muffled her shriek with kisses as he continued to thrust inward with slow, determined force, driving ever closer to her core, until at least they were joined tightly together.

He savored that moment of complete physical union, as her tight muscles clenched around him. Elizabeth trembled and panted beneath him, but he knew that their intimate ritual had just begun. He started the rhythm of mating, slowly at first, gliding back and then pressing into her inexorably, again and again and yet again.

Finally, under his ardent tutelage, Elizabeth began to imitate his movements, and the two of them jointly thrust and parted in harmony. Her hands stirred, rising to caress his strong back. Then, as his pace increased, she dug her fingers into his bottom and parted her legs wider, allowing him to thrust into her more easily. After endless minutes of delight, his hands abandoned her lovely breasts and slid beneath her to cup her pert derriere. He lifted her hips to meet him, thrust after invigorated thrust. Their sweaty bodies grew ever hotter and more flustered. Mr. Darcy concentrated on protracting their frantic union until Elizabeth reached her second peak, with a deafening scream. Her trembling muscles contracted, squeezing the length of his striving manhood with irresistible intensity. His control frayed, and he plunged forward, pounding into her in a few last, desperate strokes before reaching his own climax and filling her core with his precious, burning seed.

When they both had finally calmed and caught their breath, he rolled over to the side, not wanting to crush her. Then he pulled her into the tenderest of embraces, with her head cradled on his shoulder, their legs tangled together.

"Elizabeth, my dearest love, I have some surprising news for you. You were too distracting for me just now to reveal it."

"What is it, Fitzwilliam?"

"I have already obtained your father's permission to marry you, my love."

"What? How can that be? We only became engaged this morning!"

"In the afternoon, I sought a private meeting with your uncle and informed him that you had accepted my suit. He surprised me by saying that he had been in communication with your father, these past months, about my ... my interest in you during your stay in London, and he also told your father about my assistance to your whole family. It seems that your father found that your recent dispirited countenance rather disheartening, and so he agreed to your traveling here with your aunt and uncle. Your father and uncle had already discussed the possibility that I would ask for your hand in marriage, and so they arranged for your uncle to be able to give his consent and approval, with your father's prior permission."

"I did not know that Papa was so eager to marry me off," she said, with a shy laugh.

"I was encouraged by your uncle's replies, and so I determined that I would seek their consent to marry as soon as possible. I asked if your father had decreed how long the engagement must be, for I wished to marry as soon as you agreed. In fact, now that I have both your consent and your father's. I would dearly like for us to marry in two weeks."

"So soon?"

"Elizabeth, my love, I cannot bear to part with you any longer. I have suffered and missed you terribly, these past six months."

"What did my uncle say?"

"That he and your father had already anticipated the question, and that he could have the Longbourn church ready at any time that pleased you. As you well know, your father takes much delight in being a student of human nature, and he told your uncle that I would most likely prove to be a very impatient man."

For a moment, Elizabeth blushed and tried to retain her composure. Then she abandoned the effort, and the laughed out together regarding this remark of Mr. Bennet's.

"Yes, we are both very impatient," she conceded.

Darcy caressed Elizabeth's body and rested his hand on her abdomen. "We may as well be, since we have just anticipated our public marriage vows. Even though, privately, I have always considered you my wife, we may already have conceived a child just now, so what say you, my love? We could announce our engagement tomorrow and travel back to Longbourn in the next few days. Would that meet with your approval?"

She smiled and nodded her head in agreement, then slowly closed her eyes. It had been an exhausting and yet an exhilarating day for them both. He could sense her weariness, so he positioned her to lie close against him, then whispered sweet, loving words to her ears alone. Finally, content with the world, they drifted off to a peaceful sleep together.

\*\*\*

Meanwhile, at the other end of the house, Miss Caroline Bingley was busy preparing for a most specific ritual. The last few weeks had been extremely busy but fruitful. At the beginning of summer, she had been most unhappy when, due to health concerns, Mr. Darcy cancelled his invitation to her brother to spend time at Pemberley. She had gone to his townhouse in London, on the pretense of visiting Miss Darcy but hoping, in truth, to see the elusive man while she was there. Her attempt, however, had been unsuccessful. He did not receive any visitors. Then, not long ago, she had been alarmed to learn that her brother had decided to return to Netherfield.

Although she tried earnestly to dissuade him, she had failed in that plan, as well. He had been uncharacteristically tight-lipped about the journey, saying only that he wanted to tidy up some loose ends concerning the estate and perhaps also do some hunting.

But she was an intelligent woman. She instructed one of the servants to inform her about the goings-on in Hertfordshire. She soon learned that her foolish brother had renewed his address to Miss Bennet, and that he had, in fact, been instrumental in sabotaging Caroline's grand plan to ensnare Mr. Darcy in marriage for herself. Charles even helped to pass on a letter from the Darcys to invite that country chit, Eliza, to visit Pemberley.

Miss Bingley had been so enraged by this news that she smashed a flower vase in the morning room, upon reading that particular piece of intelligence. She was furious with both her brother and Mr. Darcy. *Who is this country upstart? My Mr. Darcy must be blind and mad to be entrapped by that impertinent nobody. She has no beauty, no wit, no manners. Her family is a shameful association. They have no connections or social status. I will find a way to make Mr. Darcy see the wisdom of having me as the mistress of Pemberley!*

Just when Caroline was practically tearing her hair out as to what to do, she had happened to overhear one of the maids talking about an all-powerful witch who could cure people of illness or capture any woman's heart's desire. She became obsessed with finding that witch and, at whatever cost, obtaining her secret assistance.

So decided, she had traveled a great distance to consult the ugly old witch, in a rather disgusting village. But the secret information she obtained from this witch were well worth the journey and the price. With careful planning, she had finally succeeded in installing herself at Pemberley, at least for a few days, at the same time as Miss Eliza. Now that she was inside the grand estate, in possession of a double package of witchcrafts, she exulted in the knowledge that she was only moments away from permanently curing Mr. Darcy of his obsession with the worthless hussy.

When midnight arrived, she spread out her precious packages on the desk. The first package contained a cloth doll and several pins. Caroline next produced a fallen hair of Miss Eliza's which she had prudently obtained during dinner, and wrapped it around the neck of the doll. Consulting the instructions on the paper given to her by the old witch, she began her chant.

She repeated it thrice: "Almighty Devil of Hell, bless me with the darkest power of evil!" Then she stuck pins into the breasts and the apex between the thighs of the doll and continued.

"Almighty Devil of Hell, bless me with the darkest power of evil! Turn this woman into a harlot! Make her wanton and compel her to pounce upon the first man she sees!"

After she completed the ritual, Caroline tidied away the evidence and reclined on her bed with a wicked smile on her face. She had not know what witchcraft she wished to obtain at first. She had simply told the witch that she wanted her rival to suffer the worst possible fate. The witch had suggested this particular evil spell, explaining that the wanton effect would only last for a few hours, or until her rival was satisfied by a man – or even more than one man.

Caroline's eyes had sparkled upon hearing the nature of the curse. Miss Eliza would be forever ruined, not just in the eyes of Mr. Darcy but in all of society. She imagined Miss Eliza waking up, wanton, with desire coursing through her body, dashing out of her room and tearing her clothes off in front of the first footman, manservant or gardener she came across.

Vastly entertained by the image, Caroline closed her eyes and drifted into a more peaceful sleep than she had enjoyed for a long while.

\*\*\*

In the master's bedchamber, Elizabeth awoke to a sudden warm sensation in her body. She did not know where she was at first. Then she saw Mr. Darcy's head on her naked bosom. Again! At last, she remembered that they had finally become one flesh.

As she remembered their first coupling, just a few hours ago, her face turned crimson. The marriage bed was very different from anything she had ever imagined or heard. Darcy's love was virile, potent and endearing. She smiled dreamily. *Perhaps the memories of our union are having an effect on me*, she mused. *I feel as if my blood is rioting around inside my body, especially around my breasts and between my legs. I feel hot.* She squirmed restlessly. *Hot and...lustful.*

She saw that Mr. Darcy was still asleep, but she needed him again, needed him urgently, without delay. Lifting one of his hands, she rubbed it hesitantly over her nipple...

It felt wonderful. His long, lean fingers grazed her sensitive nipple, enticing it to life. But she wanted more. She wanted him inside her again.

With a whimper of need, she parted her legs and rubbed herself up and down against his thighs.

Darcy startled awake at the movements against his legs. "Elizabeth, my love, what are you doing?" He raised himself and leaned on an elbow to look at her.

"I feel hot...here!" She moved his hand down to cup her womanhood. Her voice trembled, and her heart felt as if it were racing. She thought she would burst if he did not take pity and fulfill her needs now. "I woke up with a sudden warm sensation in my body, and now I feel extremely wanton. Fitzwilliam, I want you!" With a flirtatious smile, she pushed him to lie on his back, then climbed on top of him. Bending, she kissed him frantically, on the mouth, the jaw, the pulse that beat at his throat, then downward to his shoulders and chest. Straddling him more broadly, she rubbed her secret lips against his firming manhood. She uttered soft moans, and whispered incoherently as she kissed him, telling him how she loved every part of his body and how he made her feel, so very wanton and lustful.

Mr. Darcy noticed that her eyes looked dazed and unfocused, as if she were caught up in some kind of a dream, her body felt feverish against his. "Did you catch a cold this morning, my love? You are burning up!" Concerned, he wanted to press her back down on the bed so that he could fetch a doctor, and yet, with each passing moment, he was more helplessly aroused. His manhood sprang up, tall and proud, and Mr. Darcy could not deny that he was vastly enjoying the unexpected attentions Elizabeth bestowed. She continued to kiss him wildly as she tried to position herself to take his massive shaft into her. But she was still very new to the art of lovemaking, and clearly did not know how to do so.

She cried out in frustration, "Fitzwilliam, help me! I need you. Please, come inside me! I feel as if I am on fire!"

At first, he was deeply worried, but her amorous ministrations were soon too much for him to resist; he could not resist giving in to her demand. He pressed her back on the bed and entered her with one almighty thrust. Her body shook with the force of his entry, but she never wavered. Rather, she wrapped her legs around his waist and continued, hungrily, violently, to kiss him. Spurred by her ardent reaction, and urged on by her touch, he pounded into her more and more quickly, on and on, until she cried out with satisfaction. Her convulsing muscles squeezed his manhood tightly, sending him into a vortex of bliss. He howled and spilled his seed into her as he reached a powerful climax.

***

From midnight until dawn, Elizabeth refused to sleep. She was, by turns, flirty, wanton and wild with lustful needs, and he satisfied her many times, in different positions, before she finally felt the blood cease to rioting in her body. When dawn came, Darcy gently carried her back into her own bedchamber, speaking softly to her, reassuring her of his love and promising that he would care for her, not letting anything or anyone harm her. He waited by her side, sated and devoted, until she finally fell into a deep sleep.

He was, of course, still puzzled, for he knew that she had been behaving very strangely. She might yet be sick, although she no longer seemed feverish. He decided, with a belated pang of conscience, to ask Mrs. Gardiner to look after her while he sent for the doctor.

When he went in search of the Gardiners, he heard Miss Bingley giggling with her sister, around the bend of the corridor. He was ready to retreat to avoid the pair, but he froze when he heard the words being spoken in her muffled voice. "…witch gave me a special doll…make the upstart wanton…pounce on the first man she sees…will be scandalous

…until she is satisfied by the man or after a few painful hours …indeed!"

Darcy crept closer, intent on catching each vicious syllable.

"…reputation will be ruined…cannot wait to see the results…going to love seeing her complete humiliation! Mr. Darcy will be freed from his obsession with that impertinent hussy…he will see that I am the perfect mistress for Pemberley!" At that, Caroline cackled, sounding as if she herself were a witch!

Mr. Darcy, furious, wanted nothing more than to confront her and berate her for her shameful behaviour, but he realised that he did not have the luxury of doing so, for he had left his beloved alone. It was his duty to watch over her until he was sure that the last effects of the witchcraft were gone. Immediately, he returned to her bedchamber, summoned a startled maid, and requested that she bring Mrs. Gardiner to him.

He would explain only that he had overhead Miss Bingley confessing to having perpetrated some kind of evil black magic on Elizabeth, and explain that his concerns over his fiancée's health had forced him to disregard propriety and check on her, thus accounting for his presence in her bedchamber.

Even after Mrs. Gardiner's arrival, he insisted on waiting with her for Elizabeth to wake up, schooling himself to wait for the grim pleasure of confronting the villain.

An hour later, Elizabeth finally woke up. She did not feel the wanton, lustful sensation anymore, but her body ached in any number of unaccustomed places. She greeted her aunt with a sheepish look, and looked upon her beloved with a shy and shamed expression.

Mr. Darcy, breathing out a sign of relief, asked for permission to speak with her alone for a moment. When Mrs. Gardiner moved out of hearing distance, he confided to Elizabeth what he had overhead from Miss Bingley. She was horrified, but he reassured her that he was not shocked by her wanton behaviour, for he knew her to have been under some kind of evil spell or curse. He also told her, with a gleam in his eye, that he had enjoyed their night together very much. He loved her still, as ardently as ever, and they would be married in two weeks, as they had previously discussed.

Next, Darcy reassured himself that Mrs. Gardiner would not, under any circumstance, leave Elizabeth alone. He then took his leave, prepared to forcefully evict the unwanted guests from Pemberley.

## CHAPTER SEVEN

Mr. Darcy instructed Mrs. Reynolds, his housekeeper, to take care of a few things. Then he walked into the breakfast room, ready to evict Miss Bingley when a loud voice was heard.

"Where is my nephew? I must see him at once!" Lady Catherine stalked into the room, unannounced.

Darcy turned to greet her. "Lady Catherine."

"Fitzwilliam." Lady Catherine surveyed the unknown faces in the room and asked archly, "Who are all these people?"

"Have a seat and some tea, Aunt. This is Mr. Gardiner, my guest. These individuals are Mr. Hurst, Mrs. Hurst and Miss Bingley. They are relatives of my friend, Charles Bingley. Their carriage broke down near Pemberley. They are waiting here while it is being repaired, but they will be leaving very soon."

"It is a cold autumn. There is no hunting or rambling. Whyever did you invite guests to Pemberley? And what sort of people would permit their carriage break down during such weather? Your friend's relatives are most ill-planned. They should fire their head coachman. I have no time to spare for tea, for a report of the most alarming nature has reached me."

"About?" Mr. Darcy asked dryly.

His aunt bridled, still standing, but she did accept a tea cup that a brave maid offered. "Do not be facetious, young man. I was told that you are engaged to Miss Elizabeth Bennet, that young woman who had to take charity from her cousin's invitation for a visit to my illustrious Rosings. Of course, it cannot be true! But I am distressed that anyone would even compose such a fiction."

"It is no fiction," he said flatly.

"What?" His aunt recoiled. "For shame, young man. For shame! How could you even consider lowering your standards for such a woman?"

Darcy gritted his teeth. He would not allow anyone to berate his fiancée but neither would he argue with his aunt in front of everyone. "Lady Catherine, we shall discuss this in my study."

She look at him in astonishment. "I am having my tea now. Umh, surprisingly good tea, actually! Where did you procure it? I have been traveling from Kent for nearly three days, without pause. I am tired and I want answers. Simply tell me, once and for all, that it is not true."

"It is quite true. Miss Elizabeth Bennet and I are engaged, and we shall be married in Longbourn, her father's estate in Hertfordshire, in two weeks. I intend to send out the invitation to you shortly."

His aunt stiffened. "Engaged!" Her fingers tightened, and Mr. Darcy wondered whether the tea cup might shatter in her grip. "What nonsense is this? You are engaged to Anne!" Lady Catherine exclaimed.

"Engaged?" Caroline echoed. "Mr. Darcy, you cannot marry Miss Eliza. You simply cannot!"

"So soon!" Georgiana cried. "Oh, Fitzwilliam, I am so happy for you and Miss Elizabeth!" His sister sounded jubilant.

Mr. Gardiner was the only who remained silent.

"Silence, Georgiana!" his aunt thundered. "How can you congratulate your brother on such a match? This is not to be borne! The woman has no fortune and no connections. Besides, your brother is engaged to Anne. It was always the fondest wish of your mother. How can he defy the hope of his own mother? How can he ally himself with a woman of inferior birth, of no importance in the world?"

Eyeing the assembled women sternly, Darcy asserted himself. "Miss Bingley, pray mind your language. I allow no one to slander my fiancée. Aunt, pray do not speak to Georgiana in such a manner. I am sorry to contradict you, Aunt, but I never once heard my mother speak about Anne and I marrying. I have only ever thought of Anne as my cousin. I would never offer for her, for I firmly believe that our temperaments would not suit. I am in no need of Miss Elizabeth's fortune or connections. I am a gentleman and she is a gentleman's daughter. In that sense, we are quite equal."

"But who is her mother? Who are her uncles and aunts? They are merely lawyers or merchants of trade! How can you bear to link yourself with that sort of people?"

Mr. Gardiner finally spoke. "Lady Catherine, I am Elizabeth's uncle – the one who is in trade," he added wryly. "Perhaps you will not wish to continue to drinking tea, for I am responsible for its import from Ceylon. After all, you were quite clear that you do not wish to be linked with us in any way."

Lady Catherine, who had indeed been sipping the tea, nearly had it burst out from her nose. "What?" she croaked, coughing. "Fitzwilliam, how can you allow a merchant to grace your table?"

"Aunt, if you are so strict with your associations, I must ask Miss Bingley to leave the room as well, for her family's fortune was also from trade."

Miss Bingley's face turned bright red on hearing Darcy's remarks. Lady Catherine sent her a condescending glance and continued, "No wonder she dresses in so vulgar a display of fortune, with such presumed elegance. Mark my words, Fitzwilliam! This merchant woman is after your wealth and position too."

"Thank for your concern, Aunt. I consider myself to be a decent student of character, able to recognise those who are genuine in their regard for my well-being."

"Mr. Darcy, I am only looking out for your best interests. Have you forgotten that Miss Eliza was amorously involved with one of those red-coat soldiers?" Miss Bingley demanded shrilly.

"Miss Bingley, pray do not speak regarding matters about which you know nothing. Miss Elizabeth's heart was utterly untouched, except by me. Mr. and Mrs. Hurst, you have best prepare for departure. Your carriage is repaired."

"I do not care to leave just yet," Miss Bingley said smugly. "Not until I have witnessed her downfall. You will know soon enough that your so-called fiancée is no better than a harlot…"

"What a very provocative statement, Miss Bingley. Did you also hear the alarming report that someone has been trying to harm her? She began to feel unwell, last night when we were chatting together. I am happy to reassure you all that I enjoyed looking after her throughout the night, as a fiancée should – under the chaperonage of Mrs. Gardiner, of course. Miss Elizabeth had quite recovered by this morning, and I have sent Mrs. Reynolds to search for the culprits and the evidence of their misdeed. Anyone who has tried to harm her will, naturally, have to answer to me."

Miss Bingley, whose eyes had widened upon hearing Darcy's words, stood up and left the room abruptly, with Mrs. Hurst hard on her heels. Her husband, who was at a loss about what happened, nevertheless left, as well.

"You see?" Lady Catherine said witheringly. "This Miss Elizabeth brings nothing but jealousy into our midst. You would not wish to be harmed by association with her, as well." She bent her narrowed gaze on him. "Remember that there are many people dependent upon you, Nephew, and that I am your nearest relative, the closest thing you have to a mother. You are morally obliged to take my advice. If you willfully act against the inclinations of all who care about you, you will be censured, slighted, and despised. You simply cannot marry that country upstart."

"Aunt, pray do not berate my fiancée. She is the victim here, not the initiator of any trouble. Mother always said that I should choose a wife who loved me for myself, not for my position or wealth. Miss Elizabeth is charming, witty and intelligent. It has been many months since I have considered her as one of the handsomest woman of my acquaintance. And I know for a certainty that she loves me for myself, not for what the Darcy name can bring."

"Ha! How can you be so sure? She may have used arts and allurements during Easter time to blind you."

"I know for a certainty because she declined my proposal when we were in Kent."

"She refused you!" Georgiana gasped.

"What nonsense are you talking about? You proposed during your stay in Rosings?" Lady Catherine asked, looking as shocked by the locale as by the event.

"Yes. I have been in love with Miss Elizabeth since last November." Darcy could see that his declaration surprised all of the people still in the room. "But she would not have me, for all my fortune and wealth. She found me arrogant in my treatment of people in Hertfordshire, and interfering regarding the romance of Mr. Bingley and her sister Miss Bennet. It has taken me many months to prove my worth and win her heart. I will not be swayed. Miss Elizabeth and I will be married next week. If you continue to criticise her, I must ask you to leave Pemberley at once. I will not tolerate her being abused in any way, now or in the future."

"Then you are a fool! You do not know what you are getting into. Now bring me more tea and a full breakfast. I will leave for Matlock after that. Your uncle will know how to talk some sense into you."

"As you wish, Aunt. I will leave you to break your fast."

Mr. Gardiner could not help his smile. He followed Mr. and Miss Darcy out of the room, leaving the elderly lady to enjoy *his* tea.

The two men, accompanied by Georgiana, retreated to Mr. Darcy's study.

"Darcy, why was I not told about someone trying to hurt Elizabeth?" Mr. Gardiner immediately asked.

"Yes, Fitzwilliam. Is she truly well now?" Georgiana added.

"Yes, she is well now, Georgiana, but I would take it kindly if you would check on Miss Bennet for me and send Mrs. Reynolds down to us."

"Of course."

After his sister had left, Mr. Darcy continued, "I did not know about it, either, until the early hours of this morning. I believe Miss Bingley to have performed some form of witchcraft on Miss Bennet. She has recovered now and Mrs. Gardiner is with her."

"Witchcraft! What an evil woman! Do you really intend to allow Miss Bingley to leave, just like that?"

"I have asked Mrs. Reynolds to question all of their servants and to search her room, if required. Let us wait for her report."

When the housekeeper entered, Darcy looked to her immediately. "Mrs. Reynolds, did Miss Bingley's servants say anything?"

"Under the threat of being arrested for witchcraft, Miss Bingley's maid was quite forthcoming. She said her mistress went to consult a witch in an obscure village on River Orwell. She did not know what Miss Bingley obtained there, but she helped me search the room. In the drawer of the table, we found this doll, with pins stuck in it, as well as some pieces of paper with strange writing. We could not make it out, as it was almost burned to ashes, but what is left appears to be instructions on how to perform the black magic."

"Is that the only witchcraft she possessed?"

"The maid did not know, but that was the only thing we found among her possessions that looked like witchcraft. Still, the maid did tell me something about the witch. She said the woman was called Ipswich the Good Witch, famous for her good deeds and strict rules. She claimed that her curse would not work if the person did not deserve it, and that it normally had a beneficial effect on good people. And it was rumoured that evil people who asked for her spells would only get the worse end of the bargain, and would be unable to harm others ever again."

"Is that so!" Mr. Darcy was relieved by that final piece of information. "Have you asked the maid for directions to find this witch? I would like to visit her, after my wedding. I want to make sure Miss Bennet will not suffer any permanent effects from this witchcraft."

"Yes, the maid gave me some vague directions. She said that it was all she had heard about where the witch resided. The popular belief seems to be that only people who were meant to find her could succeed in doing so. But I have instructed the maid to inform Mr. Bingley if Miss Bingley should exhibit any strange behaviour."

"Good. I will send an express to Bingley about all of this."

"It seems we cannot do much more, for now," Mr. Gardiner opined. "I think I will go and check on Elizabeth."

Mr. Darcy put the doll in the safe box in the study, and then went out to see the Hursts and his aunt to their carriages. Miss Bingley, he observed, was not her usual haughty and collected self. She bumped into Lady Catherine in her rush to the carriage, and the contents of her reticule dropped out and onto the hem of the old lady's dress.

Lady Catherine brushed them aside contemptuously. "No manners at all! Your friend should teach his sister to walk properly before allowing her out in society."

Miss Bingley hurriedly collected the black candle and mirror from the ground, and dropped them back into her reticule, then favored the elderly lady with an angry glare and climbed up into the carriage.

Mr. Darcy breathed a heart-felt sigh of relief when the carriages containing his uninvited guests finally faded from view.

***

That night, dinner was a pleasant affair, all the more so because Elizabeth had sufficiently recovered her strength to join the others. With their newfound intimacy, Mr. Darcy and Elizabeth could not help constantly gazing at and whispering to each other. Mr. and Mrs. Gardiner smiled to see such love-struck behaviour.

When everyone had retired for the night, Mr. Darcy slipped into Elizabeth's room and joined her on the bed for a tight embrace.

"Are you feeling better, my love?"

She blushed and nodded. "I am fine, except for being a little bit sore."

"Where? Perhaps I can massage your sore flesh." His hands smoothed over her back.

"Fitzwilliam!"

He lowered his head and gave her a tender kiss. "I am only teasing, dearest. I know you are still too sore. And we will be leaving for Longbourn in a few days, so I do not want to completely wear you out. I simply want the pleasure of holding you, to assure myself that no lasting harm has come to you."

"I still shudder to think of Miss Bingley's witchcraft."

"Remember what the maid said about the witch. We do not deserve an evil curse, and so it had a rather different effect on us. I spent the most amazing night with you, and I loved it that you were wild for me. I was hoping to teach you how to be wanton, after we marry. This just makes my task easier."

"It is not wrong to be wanton?"

"I want you always to express your feelings freely with me, my dear. We are now of one flesh. I want you to make love to me as much as I want to love you in return."

They shared another deep kiss before drifting off together into a deep sleep.

***

In the meantime, inside the Inn of Lambton, Miss Bingley took out the black candle and mirror and spread them on the desk. She had a second package in her reticule, one which, luckily, she had left with Louisa in the morning.

She was still furious with Mr. Darcy. *How dare you send someone to go through my room! I will make your dear Miss Eliza suffer!*

She no longer had any fallen hair from that impudent upstart because of the reticule incident, but she would conduct the witchcraft anyway. She pictured Miss Eliza in her mind and chanted, according to the instruction.

"Black magic flame, dance and call upon the Devil of Hell. With your fire, make her eyes criss-crossed. With your flame, distort her nose. Devil of Hell, pray let the world see the reality of her ugly form."

After she finished the ritual, she reclined on the bed with a contented smile. If Miss Eliza had distorted eyes and nose, Mr. Darcy would soon tire of her, even if he did marry the chit.

When morning came, loud screams were heard in the Inn of Lambton. Miss Bingley woke up to find her nose twisted, like she had been punched and her eyes permanently criss-crossed. How could this have happened? It seemed without the hair of the intended victim, the witchcraft worked on the last one who touched the candle.

# CHAPTER EIGHT

An ordinary carriage drove slowly down the winding road along the river. The curtains were firmly closed, concealing the identity of the vehicle's occupants – and small wonder, for the carriage was occupied by two young gentlemen who were ardently engaged in kissing one another.

"Willie, your moustache itches!" complained the younger man wearing a hat.

"You are the one who insisted I wear a fake moustache, Elizabeth. Now you must bear with the consequences."

"Shh! Remember to call me Eli, not Elizabeth, or you shall give me away! I am much better than you in this deception. At least I remembered to call you Willie, instead of Fitzwilliam."

"I protest! Willie is a most indecent name. Call me Will or William."

Small wonder. Indeed, for the two 'gentlemen' in question were Mr. Darcy and his new wife, the former Miss Elizabeth Bennet, in disguise.

The day that Jane and Elizabeth married Mr. Bingley and Mr. Darcy in a double wedding was the proudest day of their mother's life. Although the ceremony had been arranged within the short notice of two weeks, everything turned out perfectly for Mrs. Bennet. No expense was spared by the bridegrooms, and the brides wore the most elegant silk dresses, made by an exclusive modiste in London.

Longbourn Church and the Meryton Assembly, which were used for the ceremony and the wedding breakfast, respectively, were decorated lavishly for the auspicious occasion. The breakfast included an array of expensive and exotic foods and wine that took Mrs. Bennet's fancy. She was the envy of the entire town, and actually of London and Derbyshire, as well, which was a far cry from the public pity she had received some half a year earlier when her youngest daughter was rumoured to have eloped with a red coat and then killed during a lover's brawl. Most friends and families of the couples were present, except for Miss Bingley and Lady Catherine.

Mr. and Mrs. Darcy spent their wedding night and two lazy weeks in seclusion at their London townhouse. Mr. Darcy gave most of the servants two weeks' leave, and the couple did not receive any guest for the duration. On the wedding night, he volunteered to serve as Elizabeth's lady's maid, and prepared her for the night. They did not get much sleep until late morning of the next day because the eager bridegroom wanted to prove that he could make his wife feel wanton, even without the aid of witchcraft.

He succeeded, beyond any dispute or complaint from his wife.

The late-morning awakening routine became a pattern for the first two weeks, and their blissful unions took place in nearly every room in the townhouse.

Mr. Darcy had then arranged the current trip to find Ipswich the Good Witch. He would not rest easy until he knew for certain that the witchcraft would not cause his dear wife any permanent harm. He had originally intended to part with his wife for a few days, in order to settle the matter, but Elizabeth would have none of that. She did not want him to be in danger either, and she did not want to separate from him just yet, so soon after the wedding. In the end, she persuaded him to allow her to accompany him in disguise, just as they had when they embarked upon the ill-fated search for Mr. Wickham and Miss Lydia.

Mr. Darcy enjoyed the privilege of personally binding her bosom again, taking the time to fondle and kiss her dazzling breasts. On this occasion, he also confided to her many of his wayward and more serious thoughts from their previous sojourn together in the fisherman hut. Elizabeth lightened the mood by challenging him to properly scratch his bulge and display his manly asset by sitting with his legs apart. She also teased him about his talkative drunken ramblings and his not-so-tolerable singing. Their playful banter and touches soon led to a long and tender coupling that caused their departure from London to be delayed for nearly an hour.

Midway into the journey, Darcy pulled Elizabeth to straddle his lap, and proceeded to graze her ears, cheeks and mouth with his kisses. Despite Elizabeth's protest about his fake moustache, he continued the exploration, and his hands wandered down her body.

"I forbid you to wear trousers in the future. It is most inconvenient," Darcy soon objected.

Elizabeth's eyes widened with surprise. "Fitzwilliam, you are not thinking...indeed you are not...?"

Darcy smiled devilishly. "Now who is the one who has forgotten about the disguise? And whyever could we not?"

He then pushed her away from him and pulled both his and her trousers down before hauling the stunned Elizabeth to sit back up on his thighs again, only this time facing away from him. He licked and suckled her neck and earlobes from behind. The bumpy movements of the carriage and his ministrations, as well as her own dishabille, soon excited her and made her wet. He felt her blazing heat as well. His manhood was hard and stood magnificently, demanding attention. He quickly lifted her enough to lower her onto his shaft.

The incredible sensation of having connected with her felt wonderful. He squeezed his eyes shut to savour it. After a short while, he held her waist and helped her to raise and lower her body onto him in a slow rhythm.

Elizabeth was an apt student and soon did not require his assistance. She raised her hands to hold his head firmly to her neck from behind and bounced on his thighs with vigour. She squirmed and rubbed against him when he was deep inside her. She bit her lips hard to prevent moaning out loud. This was such a novel situation to her that she soon felt the tightening of some unknown muscles. She pulled his hand to her mouth and bit onto him to muffle her cry when she reached her peak.

Darcy winced at the pain, but he was also shivering with his own needs. When she stopped the bouncing movement, he held her waist again and thrust vigorously into her from beneath. Not long afterwards, he reached his climax and buried his face against her back to drown out his own loud moans of pleasure.

After this wild coupling, the pair tidied themselves as best they could and drifted off to sleep, well-pleased with married life and with one another.

Later in the day, the carriage slowed to a stop. The couple exited the carriage and Mr. Darcy nodded to his head coachman, who was also somewhat in disguise, being dressed in less than his usual elegant clothing so that he might appear as an ordinary post driver.

Mr. Darcy and Elizabeth walked the rest of the way down the river and soon arrived at a small village which seemed to fit the description that had been wrested from Miss Bingley's maid. Darcy's men had previously scouted several villages along River Orwell before returning with reports of a possible sighting of the witch in this particular village.

The disguised couple walked along, examining the houses and shops in the small village until they came upon a depilated hut near the bend of the river. As they approached, they heard voices arguing from inside, and one of those voices sounded very like…

"Is it not Miss Bingley?" Elizabeth whispered to her husband.

"I believe so." He said.

"Should we go in or wait?"

He looked around. As the hut was in an obscured location, away from the main village, she thought it prudent to wait. So decided, he signaled for his wife to walk quietly to the side of the hut. Through the slightly opened window, they were able to hear and see what went on inside.

Miss Bingley had her hands on her hips and was shouting loudly at an elderly woman dressed in rags. The old lady was sitting in front of a small table.

"You must reverse your witchcraft! I cannot have my eyes permanently criss-crossed and nose twisted. How am I to appear in public, or attend balls, or find a rich husband? I shall be ridiculed by the ton." The angry voice of Miss Bingley was loud and clear.

"Follow the ritual or hell shall break loose. I told you that."

"I shall pay you another sum to turn me back into a beautiful woman."

"That you won't. Yer body's been touched by the Devil. No witch can handle further."

"Then I am going to kill you, you ugly old witch!" Miss Bingley screamed, and lunged onto the old lady. Outside, Elizabeth and Darcy gasped and were preparing to burst into the hut to rescue the elderly witch, but green smoke exploded from inside.

Mr. Darcy pulled Elizabeth back, away from the smoke. After they were a clear distance away from the hut, they saw Miss Bingley emerge, covered with green dust, coughing hard soon afterwards. The door of the hut banged shut behind her. As soon as she had caught her breath, she screamed and kicked at the door, continuing for a long while, until at last she was hoarse.

But her effort was in vain. The door would not open. Finally, she abandoned her futile attempts and stalked toward a boat tied farther down the river.

"What should we do?" Elizabeth asked her husband, after they saw the boat leave.

"We have come this far. Let us inquire as to whether the witch will see us."

"But what if she hurts us?"

"The maid said she was a good witch. It appears she did not hurt Miss Bingley, even after she threatened to kill her. That green smoke was probably just a diversion to force Miss Bingley out of the hut."

Elizabeth nodded and placed her hand on his, willing to trust his judgment in the matter. Together, they walked to the hut and knocked.

The door opened immediately, but nobody appeared near the door. They walked in cautiously. The green smoke had all disappeared, so they could clearly see the old lady sitting in front of the table just as she had been before -- calm and collected.

"Pray excuse us, Madam, but we are wondering if you are Ipswich the Good Witch?" Mr. Darcy asked.

"Yes, indeed. Do come forward. It is a pleasure to meet you, Mr. and Mrs. Darcy."

The couple gasped, quite surprised that she knew who they were, even in disguise.

Darcy replied, "It is also our pleasure to make your acquaintance, Madam. I believe we have something of yours which we wish to return." He took out the doll from a bag he was carrying.

"Ah, it is very kind of you to bring back the doll, Mr. Darcy. I like to reuse my materials as much as possible. It is good to the Earth for us not to be wasteful."

"Then you are aware that Miss Bingley performed the ... that wanton spell on my wife? We would be very much in your debt if you can assure us that there will not be any permanent effect upon her."

"But, indeed, sir, there will be." The old witch said.

They looked at each other and Mr. Darcy asked apprehensively, "What will it be?"

"Quite simply, the two of you will experience a forever-joyous union, well into your old ages."

The couple blushed bright red and smiled at each other. Mr. Darcy then said, "Thank you, Madam. Although I do not think we needed a spell in order to be forever blissful together."

"Perhaps not, but did Miss Bingley's maid not tell you? My magic only works on people who deserve it."

"Yes, indeed! Thank you, Madam. May I ask … what did Miss Bingley mean, when she complained that she was permanently cross-eyed and had a twisted nose?"

"She attempted to perform a second curse, but not according to the exact instructions, thus causing the curse to befall herself."

"A second curse?"

"Miss Bingley came back here a day after she obtained the first package to ask for a second curse in particular. She was worried that the first one might not work. She wanted your wife to have crossed eyes and a twisted nose. But she performed the spell without any of Mrs. Darcy's hair, so the last one to have touched the black candle bore the brunt of that second curse."

"My Lord, I had no idea that she was so vengeful. Thank you, Madam, for explaining this all to us. We will leave you now."

But Elizabeth interrupted, "Madam, is there truly no way to help Miss Bingley?"

"Bless you, Mrs. Darcy, you have a forgiving soul, in view of how badly the young woman wanted to hurt you."

"She is, after all, the sister of my husband's best friend."

"Well, I am sorry to pain you, but she bargained with the Devil when she came for the curses in the first place. She still has to bear the forfeit of the bargain."

"You are not saying…that you shall take her soul?" Elizabeth asked in a trembling voice. She had experienced so many losses and deaths recently that she could not bear to wish such a thing on even her worst enemy.

"Rest assured, I am a good witch…though a bit mischievous," the elderly witch said, and grinned, "She will not ultimately suffer for her forfeit, provided she becomes a better person. Only then will the spell of that curse be broken. Now, off you go, the two of you." The old woman then stood up and stepped into the other room.

Darcy and Elizabeth stayed in the neighbouring town for the night, for they wanted to make certain that Miss Bingley would not come back to harm the witch. But the next day, when they returned to the hut, the door stood open, and there was no sign of anything inside. It appeared that the witch had vanished.

***

**Six years later**

"Now, is it right or left?"

"Mother, you are hopeless! Come, William. We shall go and ask Papa to help her out." Five-year-old Thomas ran away from the maze, with his three-year-old brother following hard on his heels.

"Wait!" Not being able to follow her sons, Elizabeth called after them "Do not let your Father know! Ask Mrs. Reynolds to come." Elizabeth bit her lip and took a deep breath as she heard her sons running farther away, outside the maze, not even sure if they had heard her.

She had walked around the maze for a few more minutes, still without having found a way out, when Mr. Darcy suddenly appeared, a wicked grin on his face.

"Thomas and William asked me to come and rescue the damsel in distress."

She walked past him. "I did not ask for you. I asked for Mrs. Reynolds. You should go back to the guests."

He followed close behind her. "You know I cannot stand being in the same room as Miss Bingley. And by leaving, I am doing a good thing for every one in there."

"Poor Fitzwilliam, you have to bear with her horrible smelling farts!"

"The Good Witch was truly naughty! That green smoke must have been a spell, for it makes Miss Bingley pass bad-smelling gas from time to time whenever she is in the presence of rich and handsome men, and her eyes are still criss-crossed and her nose twisted. How is she ever going to find a husband? It has been like this for six years now."

"She does not fart when she is with Charles or Mr. Hurst."

"Of course not. Charles is her brother, and Hurst is not very good-looking."

"She only discharges smelly, loud gas in front of you or some of the other gentlemen. I am not entirely certain that 'rich and handsome men' are the requirements that set her off. But the Good Witch did say that Miss Bingley would not suffer, once she became a better person. I continue to live in hope."

"Perhaps she will be willing to lower her quest and settle with a poor, ugly man. Then we will not need to hold our breath around her. Elizabeth, let us not waste any more of our time discussing Miss Bingley's problems. The fragrance here in the garden is fresh, and you, my dear, smell delicious. Come here to me, my love. It is a hot summer day. You will not catch a cold. I want an article of your clothing in exchange for the next turn out of the maze."

"No. Fitzwilliam, you always detour, simply to get me as improperly attired as possible. It is broad daylight, and the children may come back. I shall try the method I learned recently, one which I read in a book. It said that if I follow the right, or the left, consistently at every turn, I shall be able to get out of any maze."

"Have you had any luck yet, following the right consistently at every turn?"

Reluctantly, Elizabeth shook her head.

Darcy chuckled. "I told the nanny to keep the children indoors. And the Bingleys are taken up with a card game. Now give me your spencer. This is not the right direction."

Elizabeth glared at her husband. He was as handsome as when they had first met, years ago. But he had become more cheerful and less reserved since their marriage. Now he leaned against the bush with his hand held out, his wicked grin spreading.

"You are certain the children will not return?"

"Yes."

"And the guests?"

"I told Bingley not to let anyone come outside."

"And the servants?"

"They have known for years not to disturb us when we are in the maze."

With those reassurances, Elizabeth walked to the next bench. She did not untie her spencer but instead slowly removed her boots and stockings, gazing at her husband all the while. She saw that his breath had become shallow, and his arousal was visible.

"See how generous I am? I offer you four articles of my clothing in one go. But I am tired of trying to find the way. You must carry me out of this bothersome maze."

He walked over and settled her on his lap. "Delighted, my little hussy! But only after I have thoroughly rewarded myself first. You know, you have become heavier after bearing three children."

Elizabeth smacked his chest and said, "Insufferable man! You are the one responsible for ruining my figure."

"Who said your figure is ruined? I love every inch of your voluptuous body."

He then untied her spencer and pushed it – along with her gown – off her shoulders. Then he feasted on her creamy bosom, acting much like their hungry infant daughter, suckling and squeezing Elizabeth's twin peaks.

In turn, she untied his breeches and mounted him eagerly, bouncing and rubbing against his hard body. They rocked together for a long while, moaning in delight and savoring the blissful sensations of their rhythmic dance, until they reached their peak together. Nearly two hours passed before Mr. and Mrs. Darcy finally departed from the maze to return to their guests.

Nine months later, another little Darcy was born. Thankfully, he did not inherit his mother's poor sense of direction, despite having been conceived within the heart of the maze. As for Miss Bingley, after another three years of frustrated striving, she finally agreed to wed a rich, not-so-handsome elderly gentleman in trade, much to the relief of her relatives.

To

Lavender Girl, thank you for inspiring this story
Theresa Jean, thank you for your constant support

LaVergne, TN USA
15 January 2010
170093LV00004B/1/P